Pieces for a Glass Piano

PIECES FOR A GLASS PIANO

Majella

GERARD LEE

1/1

University of
Queensland Press

Published by University of Queensland Press,
St. Lucia, Queensland, 1978

© Gerard Lee, 1978

Typeset by Academy Press Pty. Ltd., Brisbane
Printed and bound by Silex Enterprise & Printing Co.,
Hong Kong

Distributed in the United Kingdom, Europe, the
Middle East, Africa, and the Caribbean by Prentice-
Hall International, International Book Distributors
Ltd., 66 Wood Lane End, Hemel Hempstead, Herts.,
England

*National Library of Australia
Cataloguing-in-publication data*

Lee, Gerard Majella, 1951—.
  Pieces for a glass piano.
  ISBN 0 7022 1169 9.
  ISBN 0 7022 1175 3 Paperback.

  I. Title.

A823'.3

to the spirits of Rosecliffe Street

Contents

Acknowledgments

Some of these pieces have appeared before: in *Meanjin, Makar, Ear in a Wheatfield, Three Blind Mice Annual, Dodo, Riverrun,* and *The Cane Toad Times.*

FRAGILE
ECCENTRICS

AJAX and the Dunny Van

I'm sitting in the cabin of this guy's Mack and I'm
scared of saying the wrong thing, afraid to speak
cause I know that as soon as I open my mouth he'll
know something's up. Already I can feel the red tape
hanging out the corner of my mouth. When you pull
that red tape, out comes a uni degree and it's got
my name on it.

"Hey what the fuck's this? What's this crap,"
he'd ask, looking at me.

I'd be speechless. Yes, he'd given a ride to someone
who'd studied Old English, Hindu civilization,
Buddhism, Ancient Rome and Greece, the works of
Tacitus, Herodotus, Socrates, et al. I'm sure he'd
be very interested in them. He'd think about Socratic
dialogue and Platonic love as he changed tyres. Can't
remember his name—Col, Terry, Dennis—some
fair dinkum ocker name. Truckies are good men to
know as long as you're up in the cabin with them.
Any other way, they're bastards. This guy was
giving me a lift to Hellawell, in the heart of
backward Queensland. And you'd be surprised at
what goes on there.

When you make it to Hellawell, you've got to watch your p's and q's, you've got to sling them around carelessly as if you're one of the boys. Bring up Plato or Socrates and they'll bring up their beer. Hellawell's an open cut coal mine, set up by the Mormon dominated Utah Development Company. And I tell you, they don't want any wise guys there.

It may please a Mormon to look at that coal field from God's angle. What he'll see is a huge area (hundreds of square kilometres maybe) dug up like turfs out of a lawn and tiny machines groping round in the gravel underneath.

First day in the kitchen, I realized it was better than most places to work, cause you were out of the sun. They put me on washing pots and mopping floors. I didn't mind. I'm not one of these guys with a uni degree who gets bitter because he has to scrub floors; not when I'm raking in nearly three hundred a week, plus board and keep.

They didn't kill you with work, but the cook was Bavarian and to keep him happy (or as close to it as he ever got) you had to look like you were working all the time. If he caught you slacking, he'd poke his finger at benches and yell, "Ajack! Ajack! Ajack!" which meant you had to clean them with Ajax. I didn't have a degree for nothing.

So, we'd clean the benches for the tenth time that day. But who cared. I admired him, he was the best chef I'd ever met. Three times a day he brought forth what looked like a home-cooked meal, for two hundred miners. And they'd slouch in like a pack of greasy apes, covered in oil and coal. The rugged look was very popular at Hellawell, grease on the face, coal on the boots. They'd look at the kitchen staff as if we were just a bunch of poofters in white.

The Bavarian chef didn't flinch when they'd come in, crunching coal into the polished tiles, leaving big greasy thumb prints on his plates. He had standards to keep. But to do it, he had to down two dozen stubbies a day, plus a couple of bottles of vodka each night. I never saw him eat a thing except a few slices of braun with his beer.

After a week in the kitchen I was sacked. I hadn't spoken a word about Hinduism or discussed the influence of Milton on modern cartoons, nothing like that.

"I'm going to have to finish you up."

"Yeah, why," I said, wringing the detergent from my hands.

"You just don't fit in."

What can you say to that?

"Finish up tomorrow."

I went back to the sink. "You just don't fit in . . . you just don't fit in . . . " echoing in my head. Shit! I can't mix with your normal Aussie. Was it because I didn't sink piss? What kind of snobs were they?

At lunch time I ate quietly, told Sam I'd been sacked.

"Why mate?"

I didn't want to say. There were two other kitchen hands sitting with us. I'll call them Ernie and Jim. Jim was Irish, a real leprechaun. He watched me from under a twisted eyebrow, a sneaky, mean, green eye. The trouble was I'd ignored one of the most sacred laws and Jim'd dobbed me in.

The night before, I'd gone to the movies. After finishing the pots early, I skipped out the back door. That morning Jim had a word to say.

"We work as a team here mate. You finish early, you come and help me and Ernie. We finish early, we come and help you. We work as a team here."

Then he erupted into this funny laugh and looked at me, "I've never known such a lazy bastard, ha ha ha."

I just laughed too, but I noticed he and Ernie never did finish early. Everyone else on the staff always had to give them a hand. Ernie was ex-army, the type who can look busy doing up his fly. What a master he was.

So they were my undoing, or so I thought. But all was not lost. The other blokes put in a good word for me during the night, and next day, I was re-instated. A second chance! For a few days, they saw me as a changed man but Jim was still having his joke about me being the laziest bastard he ever knew. One morning I'd had enough.

"Working hard?" he asked in passing, trying to kick over my mop and bucket and make it look an accident.

"Look Jim, I don't like the way you joke about that. I work as hard as . . . ."

He exploded. "Right boy, come in ere."

He strutted into the garbage room and shaped up. It was like a boxing ring. "I'll have you any day."

"I don't believe in fighting, Jim, you know that."

I looked down, trying to adopt a pacifist pose.

"Carm on yew bastard."

"Stop saying I'm lazy that's all."

"What's it got to do with you? I got my work you got yours."

I could see it was difficult to be logical with such a man. He relaxed however. I walked out and started mopping again.

After that, I found myself doing most of the harder jobs, onion peeling for hours, weeping, cleaning out the potato-chip machine, the garbage room, unloading meat, and, worst of all, making braun from boiled pigs' head. I'll never forget those pig brains! The leprechaun kept his distance, watching me out of the corner of his eye.

The camp manager was also Irish, Donovan was his name. But a simple mispronunciation gives you Dunny Van. Why did I call him that? Because. Have you ever met anyone who fits perfectly into a category, the archetype of that category? You know, like a perfect, dead ringer galoot, a tool-head, a wombat, or galah. Well Dunny Van was an archetypal poonce. It's hard to pin down the characteristics but I'll have a go:

(a) a tight little bum, that sticks out and wiggles;

(b) a nasal grating voice:

(c) a fussy hair-do;

(d) easily riled but ineffectual personality.

That was Dunny Van. He hated the way I sang "Danny Boy"—at the top of my voice.

I got the big tip off. Someone overheard Dunny Van saying, "He thinks I can't sack him, thinks he's got the staff onside, but he'll go."

I must hand it to him. That poonce could pick a uni degree from a mile off. Nothing I could do to camouflage it.

Do you know what it's like to be working at a job, knowing everyone's just waiting to see you drop through the despatch trap-door? Everyone else knows where it is, they step over the sensitized area by habit. A degree doesn't help a bit. All you know is that one day you'll take that long and sudden drop. It makes you sing "Danny Boy" so much louder —you sing it in a wild frenzy, while you're mopping the mystery-ridden floor.

One afternoon Sam and I were unloading meat. We'd been working for hours. Both of us were tired. I'd just picked up a thirty pound pack of liver, thinking of Portnoy. As I put it down, I felt something snap in my groin. This was it. The ultimate work experience—a hernia. Jesus it hurt. I lay there on the floor of the freezer looking through frosty plastic bags at great red lumps of t-bone. What comfort they afforded me.

The ambulance man came. He'd invited me to his hut the night before but the blokes told me he had some strange habits so I gave it a miss. And now, here he was, holding onto my balls as they began to turn to brass in the cold of that meat freezer.

By mistake, I was driven to the lady doctor at Dysart. I thought it'd be nice to see a lady. I watched her sterilizing herself before touching a kitchen-hand's balls and noticed her legs looked like they were covered in some kind of lizard skin. She handled my little sack but it gave me no thrill and I reckon it's safe to say she got none either.

Easier work after that, just bench scrubbing and potato peeling. It left me plenty of time for mischief. By the fourth week, I was like a kamikaze kitchen-hand. Paranoia had me on a meat hook. I knew my days were numbered. Dunny Van never spoke to me but watched everything I did. He needed evidence. I was masochistic in the way I fed it to him.

In the dining room was a notice about what movies were showing. So the miners' wives'd ring the cook to find out what was on. It drove him crazy. Burr . . . burr . . . "Hello!" he'd yell like a command into the phone. Then we'd watch as his cheeks puffed up and steam issued from his ears. He'd slam down the receiver and strut away clenching his fists. Then he'd mimic a high, delicate, polite voice.

"What's on at the pictures tonight?" with a mean little smile on his face. It only lasted a split second before he really lashed out.

"Fucken movies. Zey ring me up . . . . What's on at da movies? Fuck zem. What zey sink zis iss, a fucken information counter."

As soon as he'd cooled down, Sam or I would slip away to a booth just outside and ring up again with the same question. He'd go beserk. We could hear him from outside.

"Blah, blah, blah, Fuck zem, blah . . . ."

He'd have had our brains for braun if he'd known. Other times we'd ring up and ask for Jack. This was virtual suicide. I shook so much I could hardly slip the coin in when I made those calls.

"Hello, Jack there?" I'd say.

"Jack? Jack who?"

"Ajack!"

I thought he'd drop the phone, grab his meat axe and come straight through the wall at us, but his brain was too fuddled and pickled. He just couldn't get the joke. He must have been on automatic while he cooked those fantastic meals. No other way could it be done.

And Jim the Irishman was a target. T-shirts with any writing or pictures on them were his pet hate. He thought they were just for posers. On the other hand, his obsession was brilliant shining table tops. I'd wipe them down once, he'd come straight after me and do it again, sneaking a look at me now and then, re-positioning every ashtray. Mister Sheen we called him. One afternoon, before he came on duty, I finger-printed Mr. Sheen onto his wonderful white t-shirt. Later on I rang with an Irish accent and got him on the phone. I knew this was really pushing it. But I was desperate for revenge and ready to run.

"Mr. Sheen?" I inquired politely.

"Who?" he said.

"Clean, clean Mr. Sheen."

That's all I could handle, I dropped the receiver and bolted. Nothing came of it.

Nothing directly. The next pay day I found a note in with the crisp twenties. It was Dunny Van talking. "To bring staff requirements into line it's necessary you become redundant. Finish work next Thursday."

That was it, the final notice. Nothing could save me now. Still, I was ready to leave, it was what I wanted. What amazed me though is that Dunny Van only spoke to me once, when I first met him. After that, everything between us was via the media of the other kitchenhands.

My last morning in the kitchen was just as a customer. Pleasant to have your back pocket bulging with dough and to be on your way home. The chef took me aside. Apparently he didn't have anything to do with my sacking.

"Look, you good fella. No hard feelings eh? We meet outside we go and have a drink together. Come in here. I'll fix you somezing for ze trip." (Notice how he said "outside"—as it we were in jail.)

He took me aside, loaded me with nuts and apples and pieces of cold chicken. I stood there accepting it all, feeling like a real bastard for the way I'd annoyed him.

Outside, I waited by the petrol bowser for a lift. The first car that stopped looked like a dunny van. You can guess who was driving.

Fear and Loathing in West End

It should be a tradition. When the young man leaves home and family, he should purchase a new pair of shoes. I can see it all now, "Steppin Outs—for young hopefuls". By their shoes you shall know them.

The first Saturday after leaving home I bought a pair of sneakers that had a mind of their own. They were on my feet before I left the shop. It felt great to be walkin. That keep-on-truckin feeling. All I wanted for now was a piece of temperate fruit.

Temperate fruit, that's the stuff when you're crisp and sparky. An apple or a pear. Shoo do ah, shoo do ah, steppin out for an apple or pear. Then, all of a sudden, my feet were bouncing across a very clean part of the footpath. (West End's noted for its sidewalk slag and dog droppings. I'd hit a patch you could eat your breakfast off. It was just outside a temperate fruit shop.)

There they were, a pyramid of shining yellow pears and beside them a neat little greengrocer, trim and smooth, short with well-groomed black hair.

Smile crinkles at the edges of his eyes. Or that's what I thought they were.

I like picking my own fruit. It's bad enough that you can't pull it off trees. I grabbed a couple of pears from the pyramid and dug into the pocket.

"Forty cents boy."

Forty cents! Quite a price for a couple of pears (in those days anyway). But they were like gold, I'd have paid a fortune for one of them. My shoes were still bouncing under me like springs and that loosened my tongue, so this is what I said:

"Pretty pricey pears you got." Ha ha.

Have you ever noticed how smile crinkles can turn into vicious squints? This little chappie had those ambiguous lines. He gave me the evil eye. He aimed his finger at me. I started to wobble on my springy sneakers.

"Where you come from boy?"

Jesus! I expected a black Mafia limousine to slide into the kerb.

"Eh? Where you come from boy?" His sharp brown eyes piercing me.

"Ah ah . . . Dutton Park." (It's a nearby suburb.)

"Well . . . you get back there, we don't want you boys round here."

I backed away. I paced off quickly, hoping I wasn't being followed by one of the West End boys. It took the fun out of shopping. For a time, I didn't dare go near West End.

Migrants have a hard time I suppose. A friend of mine, when he was old enough to know better, used to stir this particular fish shop owner. He'd run in with a friend and they'd both say quickly, "den cents worda chips zmate". Then they'd be gone and the owner after them, hurling full bottles of Coca-Cola. One day they made it to their car but couldn't start it. It's guys like my friend who'd drive anyone insane.

Eventually I did return to the Mafia run, and this time, while trying to zip past the shop, noticed the almost chrome finish on the footpath outside. No one in the shop except that darty little sprite polishing something. He seemed to recognize me but I wasn't in a temperate fruit mood.

On my next visit to his pyramids I was in company with Lindy. She was one of the girls in the house where I was living. A small but fiery character, and nice.

You know how girls are when they go shopping. Businesslike. They rake through tables with bargain shoes or shirts on display. They can tell a shop assistant "no, I don't like that", or "no, that's not me". The shyest women blossom into confident shoppers. Lindy's confidence had a chrome finish.

We were strolling through West End and suddenly she veered off into the Mafia shop. No time to warn her. As usual, there was nobody in the place except Little Mr. Neat, his eyes glinting, his arms akimbo. The fruit was beautiful, shining there under the mirrors; Lindy went to the back where bundles of beans were neatly displayed, carrots arranged in order of size, pumpkins cut open cleanly, Glad-Wrap everywhere. She had picked up a few of the bean bundles and thrown them aside before the Hit Man got to us. By then, I had passed through panic and entered a malicious vacuum, where I waited (as passive as possible) to see the confrontation.

He approached very close and watched her for a while, his eyes shining so much I could have sworn he was burning inside. She looked up and saw him. Her dark eyes and his. Still looking at her, he replaced every package as it had been, not saying a word. His eyes were shining like black cherries. I was hoping for something better. It was pretty uncomfortable, but eventually she backed out of the shop and I followed. When we were a little way down the street she looked at me and said: "He's off the planet!"

I replied: "It must be a front, like that brothel in Melbourne Street with the big fish-n-chip sign. The only fish you'd get in there wouldn't come in breadcrumbs."

She looked at me with an amused reprimand as if to say, "don't be rude". She often lapsed into the female stereotype.

"He's like a bower bird," she said.

Just a night or two later, Lindy and I were driving home about midnight, through West End. As the car was coming up adjacent to the shop, I saw something shining on the footpath. Moving closer, we saw him, on his hands and knees, polishing the chrome where it curved down over the gutter.

We both just stared at each other and you know, maybe we fell in love there and then.

A Visit to
My Chiropractor

My Uncle Wal is a potato man. Not that he's a vegetarian ("rabbits" he calls them), no, he keeps his amorphous mass bulging with beer and steaks. But he's a potato man in that he looks like a potato.

When we were kids, my brother and I used to dress up potatoes with big paper collars and ties, then kick them round the backyard. There's an Uncle Wal! BLAM! POW! ZAP! It was one of our best games. The sun would go down with the broken heads of Uncle Wal lying all over the grass. Like voodoo I suppose. I've got an Uncle Wal on the desk now, with knives and screwdrivers and pins etc. embedded in his bloody skull. The bastard!

Uncle Wal is an insurance broker. At weekends he comes shooting ("anything I can get into my sights") in the country round here.

Uncle Wal on Chiropractors:
"I wouldn't insure any bastard who goes to one a those bone crunchers."

It's early Friday morning, Uncle Wal at my front door telling me I look like the hunchback of Notre Dame.

"No, I wouldn't Uncle Wal."

"They'd kill a man!" he roars. "And as for that fella in town. The most charitable thing to say about him is that he's weak wristed."

I long for the days when I was a bouncy lad kicking Uncle Wals round the yard and eating the Cadbury's block he brought with every visit. Down on the road I see his Landcruiser stacked with shotguns, ready for his three-day weekend.

"Meet you at the Commercial for a countery," he says, slaps me on my twisted spinal column and leaves me on the floor, frothing at the mouth with the pain of it all.

Lunch with Uncle Wal is okay if your back's in good shape and you can somehow manage to turn your whole body into an ear. You know, change bone to grissle and your flesh into that eary embryonic shape—for listening. But at the moment all I want to do is to get my vertebrae slipped back into their comfortable niches.

I make an appointment with Hans, the chiropractor. I think about a joke in which I call him Wrists. Funny, eh?

The Mystery of the Parallel Dints:
If you were in the habit of standing on the street outside the chiropractor shop you'd have seen many

customers file out with two parallel dints running up their faces. AND if you were in the habit of sitting in the butcher's next door, you would have heard many meat-eating customers ask Mr. Penfold.

"I think there's funny goings-on in that chiro-place. Why's everyone got dints on their faces when they come out?"

And for the umpteenth time that day you would have seen Mr. Penfold shrug, wiggle his short moustache, and then bring down that meat cleaver like one possessed.

My Chiropractor, Someone like Adam:
"I come from the Stream of Life, I am in the Stream of Life and when I was created and spun out into orbit, the whole Stream of Life consulted itself. I have been forever. I am spinning now in orbit like so many other beings and each of us gives out an influence, which spreads and crosses with other influences. My influence is formed by what I eat but most people are receiving my influences into a Bacon and Egg Consciousness. Do you eat good food?"

Those words are from the mouth of Hans, himself. In answer to the question I hum and harr and before I can explain my simple theory on food, he's off again.

"You see, the Bacon and Egg Consciousness feeds on itself. Heavy food needs energy to digest it so Stomach says, give me more, more steak, more bacon and eggs."

I listen. Sometimes I think I'm too passive. I lie there on his bench like a hunk of meat, my jocks guarding the last bastion of modesty.

Hans is a small, very energetic man. He's what I'd call a chap. I check out his wrists for limpness. They look okay. His eyes are large and blue, his hair black and curly. He's wearing red corduroys and riding boots, no shirt. The boots are a bit of a worry.

On his wall is the largest picture I've ever seen of an eye. It's an iridology master chart. That eye exerts a magic on me as Hans firmly massages my back. He seems to linger at times on the buttocks. Uncle Wal's great boofhead comes to mind. Maybe he's right. Wal's a down-to-earth person, uses his nouse, his commonsense. I check out the shop for whips and other erotic devices. All clear.

Hans has a persistent voice and his fingers perpetrate a kind of power over me. Suddenly, he is silent. At the same time, he holds firmly two bones at the base of my skull. I go into a kind of trance. Fears of being raped are present but I can't relate them to myself. I don't even care to cover my buttocks. Then he lets me go. Talks again.

"Did you have any trouble finding the place?"

"No. Someone told me it was next to the butcher's." I chuckle. He mentions the malignant effects of meat.

I relax under his hands, my mind wanders outside to stand on the footpath in the sun, watching people crowd into the butcher's, feeding the Dead Flesh Consciousness.

He rubs me some more and asks me to sit up. Immediately, he has me in a half-Nelson. He jerks my head forward and my whole spine cracks. This is only the beginning.

"Trust me," he says confidentially. "On your side."

I obey. He holds my hips one way, my shoulders the other and looking down on me, like a wrestler, he says, "Trust me, I'm good, I have to be to survive here."

And saying thus, jerks down sharply. About sixteen vertebrae go into a spasm of cracking pain from which I recover surprisingly quickly. I'm tingling.

"Sit up!"

I did, and my backbone was as supple as a snake's. I unravelled to my full height. Beautiful!

"You don't trust people eh? You're like me. What star sign are you?"

I don't answer. I'm wondering how a man who talks so much can at the same time make me feel like Elvis on stage.

"What star sign are you?"

"Faeces!"

He thinks that's funny.

"You're welcome to stay for lunch."

"Thanks."

But I can't wait to get my lips around the chocolate bar I've hidden in my pocket.

*

Lunch:

We have it like a picnic on the carpeted floor of his office. A hippie-looking friend of his named Garry is there to join us. Garry's complexion is smooth and clear. I'm so ashamed of my Violet Crumble resting heavily against my leg like an unwanted erection.

A Lesson in Sandwich-making:

Hans has a special method to make sandwiches. It's based on his concept of food. He puts a flagon on the carpet and I think, "ha, a European, he knows how to live, he'll have a drop of white with lunch", but no, it's a flagon of oil, some of which he pours onto a slice of granular Dr. Vogels. He is an energetic sandwich-maker. He has to be to maintain control over his materials. He piles slices of tomato and cheese onto the bread and then adds a huge amount of lettuce. That sandwich was about ten inches high, and eight of them were lettuce. He noticed me looking.

"I believe that eighty per cent of our food should be alkaline-forming, so, the lettuce."

And with that, he wacked his jaws around it savagely.

"I've been living with a cancer for the last year," says Garry.

"A cancer?" I'm concerned.

"Yes, my girlfriend's a Cancer."

"Beautiful," said Hans through the sandwich,

"but you have to be very nice all the time, never get upset . . . calm . . . "

"Right! Right!"

By this time I was pouring the oil onto the slice of Dr. Vogels, but peeling a Violet Crumble in my secret impure mind.

"I lived with a Cancer once," said Hans. "That was my wife, for sixteen years. Ah, but I like to be free, come and go. I've been with a Pisces, a Scorpio, an Aries, very passionate the Aries."

"Right!"

"Ah . . . it's good to try them all out."

What am I missing out on? I piled on the lettuce.

"Garry, heard about you getting into malteds and cream buns after the fasting you did with me."

"Yeah. First thing I did when I got back to Melbourne was to buy a deal . . . smoked it all myself. Oh Hans."

Oh Jesus! I see Uncle Wal through the curtain, walking down the main street, with a rifle and two dead rabbits over his shoulder. He thinks he's in a Western.

"But you're still vegetarian?" asks Hans.

"Oh yeah. Of course!" says Garry.

I feel the chocolate now, assuming immense proportions. It grows on me like a tumour. Uncle Wal sits grandly on the seat just outside Hans's shop. I watch him through the curtain but I'm sure he doesn't know I'm here. I'm still wondering what to do, when I notice an elderly woman crossing the street. Her head is on one side, as if it's been tied down to her left shoulder. She knocks on the door.

Hans calls out "come in".

As soon as she opens the door I know I'm done for. I'm looking straight at that potato man with the rabbit carcasses hanging off his huge frame. He fixes me with his eyes and comes to the door.

"Well what's this? Some kind of poofter's picnic?"

Garry and Hans, and the old lady with the neck tied down, are non-plussed. They can't take their eyes off the dead rabbits.

I apologize and leave quickly. Later as I search my pocket for the Violet Crumble, it's not there. I must have dropped it. Jesus!

The Parallel Dints Phenomenon Explained:
"What are those parallel dints on your face?" asks Uncle Wal on the way to the Commercial. I rub them trying to erase the marks of shame.

"Nothing, they're just from a slot in his bench; you put your face in it so you can breathe . . . Hans is good. He's made me feel like Elvis Presley."

With that, Uncle Wal takes me under his huge arm, "Yeah, I didn't mind Elvis. You know he had a $2 million insurance policy with our American branch."

"Yeah?!"

Fud! Fok!
and Other Derivations

It's tonight. Tonight's the night Fitz'll get his balls knocked in. Like a bull at a gate. But he was never any different. He'll learn.

And he says to me, "yer brain's in yer bum". By that he means I learn everything from books. He'll learn. He'll be back here tonight with a fist full of twisted testes. That's if he makes it back.

He's gone to the Homestead to "crack on to a chick". Eccentric bastard! His brother's the same, though a slightly different version. Bikie molls think he's Prince Charming. And his line is "you know, I think I really love you". It's pathetic isn't it? But it sucks them in. They immediately metamorphose into soft caring mothery creatures. And he laps it up like milk.

Fitz's more independent, he's got ideas, and unfortunately his ideas lead him to believe in this introduction: "I wanna fuck your cunt." That's simple enough isn't it? God help him!

It all started with Geoffrey Chaucer. Chaucer has a way with words, he can use a seven-letter word (shortened these days to the infamous four) and make it sound like poetry. See the Muses touching the cesspool of his mind, letting loose a school of blue sacred fish, flowing down his pen and onto the page as these lines:

> And prively he caughte hire by the queynte,
> And seyde, "Ywis, but if ich have my wille,
> For deerne love of thee, lemman, I spille."

The Miller's Tale

Quaint eh?

Fitz's got a way with words too but they don't sound like poetry. That's why he'll arrive back here tonight with a squeaky voice.

Few people (in Queensland anyway) can hear the word "cunt" without recoiling a little. Fitz reckons he can but it's all show, his stomach's corroding away with guilt. I have trouble, not that I blush, it's just a distaste. The problem is, up here, it's used purely as an insult. The same with "fuck", always a verbal dagger, full-blooded lips curled back in the heat of the moment.

I'd really love to live in Sydney or Melbourne, in cultured circles, you know, where writers and experimental film-makers and ad-men and you know, everybody, come together and have intercourse using those words with regard to their true etymology. What a buzz! e.g. "O Julia, you know I really enjoy fucking you."

But up here, it's so hard to be sophisticated. Julia would knee you in the groin. Fitz and I, we're both purists, always aspiring to the highest and best. But it's hard. God knows, I've tried to find an earthy sensuality in those words, repeating them over and over I don't know how many times. I say them sweetly, poetically, but they never change.

Last week, I was at a stage where "cunt" was beginning to assume a moist luxury, the mound of Venus, a ripe fruit, etc. That very night a bloke leaned out of a bus window and called me a cunt. Drunk of course, the saliva dripping out of his mouth. The back of that bus disappeared like some great fathead, short back and sides, spewing up dust. That's the type of conditioning Fitz and I have to fight against. Help me Chaucer!

I took myself to the *Oxford English Dictionary* in the Queensland Public Library eager to discover something beautiful at the roots of obscenity. It was a 1933 model Oxford, probably the last one that didn't have "fuck" listed. The librarians watched me as if I was a schoolboy looking up dirty words. But maybe that's just paranoia. I tell myself I'm a scholar, a Scholar.

I tried *Webster's New Twentieth Century Dictionary of the English Language*, Unabridged, Second Edition, based upon the broad foundations laid down by Noah Webster, extensively revised by the Editorial Staff, under the general supervision of Jean L. McKechnie, including etymologies, full pronunciations, synonyms, and an encyclopedic supplement of geographical and biographical data, scripture names, foreign words and phrases, practical business mathematics, abbreviations, signs and symbols, weights and measures, forms of address, but no "fuck".

The closest I could come was "fud" derived from the modern German form of abuse "Hundsfott", meaning buttocks. Oh bum!

It reminded me of a note Fitzy left when I wasn't at home one night: "I came, I saw, I threw up. Fok!" You can see from this note that deep down he's fairly prudish and doesn't like to actually spell out the more popular form.

The dictionary contained other suggestive words like "fucus"—a water weed used to make rouge. Can you see the ladies leaning down to pluck the weed with nimble fingers, floating underwater, white arms reflected on the surface. "Fucus" was used in 1675 by a guy named Cocker: "Virtue hates fucus." And well it does cocko. Fitzy'd use it like this: "Fucus will ya?"

Then there was "fubsy" meaning fat; "fucaceous", of seaweed; and to "facate" meaning to beautify with rouge, hence disguise. But no "fuck".

I followed a hunch and looked up "occupy". Feeling flushed, I glanced round; those librarians, Guardians of the Word, modern sterile Muses. Fitz told me "occupy" used to mean sexual intercourse way back in medieval days.

> King Arthur: "Sir Lancelot, I want that occupying dragon dead before noon."

In actual fact, in 1340 a writer who sported the name Hampole used the word but not in the way you'd expect. Makes you wonder what he did to deserve such a distinguished surname. The 1933 Oxford said the origin of "occupy" hadn't been ascertained. "Fud!", I said to myself, "if I was in

Sydney and Melbourne now, the librarians would give me a ball to ball on all those sort of words. Fud!"

Fitz's delved a fair bit into slang in the Australian language and he's tried for hours to make those two little words metamorphose, even just in his own mind. He tried repeating them too, "but they just get fucken worse mate".

Still he believes that buried deep down in them, as in the depths of a well, the Muses laze erotically in a watery world, their large legs carelessly open, revealing the treasure of their full bodies. I've heard him argue like this:

"Look mate, we've gotta get a new under-fucken-standing of the four-letter word. We gotta sophisti-cate ourselves. If they can do it in Sydney and Melbourne, we can do it here."

"I know Fitz, but . . . ."

And then he tells me again about the time he was in a bar in Sydney and the barmaid was so beautiful, blond, "spoke like a queen without the plums mate, no plums just perfect accent . . . and she said 'fuck', mate the way she said it . . ."

He drifts away repeating to himself the word, like a mantra, trying to say it exactly the way she did. I can see it in his eye how slowly she undresses him, takes him firmly by the hand, hurries him away through dark waters, whispers sweet "nothings" in his ear. Come back Fitzy!

But Fitz is right, you can't resurrect the four-letter word unless you use it in context, in conversa-tion, I mean language is a social thing, a communication. It has to be used publicly. It doesn't work to sit in your room repeating "fuck". We've both tried that. "You get randy as a rabbit mate, end up jerking off. Look. That Sydney lady was neck deep in sensuality and innocence. She's probably never heard anyone referred to as a cunt. Not her."

Right again. Recondition our everyday speech. We can't afford to slip up just to let off steam. They're sacred words. Sacred. So here I am reading Chaucer trying to make them sound poetic while Fitz has gone off for the big kill. An ambitious lad. There he is trying to purify the language and what'll happen to him . . . "Life's a cunt", I say to myself, "And a pity it wasn't," Fitz once retorted, forever on the look-out for slip-ups. I try to imagine how he'll sound with a squeaky voice.

I can see him now walking round at the Homestead, bow-legged and stumbling, trying to crack on to the nurses there, being laughed at. Then he'll see her, a vision in black velvet. A little Lady. Plenty spunky. Her thick golden hair exuding mysteries of depth and warmth, flowing down to where her waist aches to be captivated by a long strong arm. Fitz has that very arm on him at that moment. He approaches her innocently like a huge wooden puppet, the voluptuous Muses holding the strings, lays bare to her the passionate language of his dark watery soul.

"Wad jew say to her?" His neck's in a vice.

"Don't Joey, he didn't mean it. Did you?"

How can a man back down now? What can he say? No?

"Well look I did mean it in a way, it's just . . . "

"Pissorf crud!"

As he ambles off rubbing his neck back to life he hears behind him "k'nidiot", the unkindest cut. The nurses are snickering too. Then the cops'll get him and bash his balls in just to teach him some manners. I feel for him, try to pull my own balls inside.

The Muses could bring him home safely but my prayers can't reach them. I can't say the words with absolute purity. I've never been to Sydney to learn. Those ladies are too cool.

I remember him at the front fence, just a few short hours ago, just a bit of a kid.

"Mate, come on let me go, it's the only way, the real way," he said as I tried to wire him to the gate.

But he was off, into the panelvan, roaring into a highway of darkness where the Muses floated in the deep night sky, luring him to a watery grave.

I return to the pleasures of *The Canterbury Tales* and I'm almost finished when I hear the roar of the panelvan, the extractors throbbing. The name on the tailboard "Fish", with scales spray-painted along the sides.

I answer the door.

"Gedday mate, I'd like to introduce Bernice. She's from Sydney."

"Hi."

COASTING

Nirvana

I've envied a permanent wheelchair victim. I have.
It's not that crazy when you realize
  (a) the wheelchair was a little motorized job
  (b) on the back hung a neat insulated drinking
      bottle, ready for him to have a sip anytime
      he wanted
  (c) the victim had a smile on his face
  (d) he was chugging happily by the window
      behind which I worked as a temporary
      clerical assistant.
What's going on here I said to myself trying to be
jolly. You're envying a paraplegic! But friends, it
was just another case of the Greener Grass Syn-
drome.

He looked so happy, and, when you think,
everything'd be done for him. All he'd have to do
would be to sit down all day and press a button for
a change of scene. Don't call me callous, have pity
for Christ's sake on a poor filing clerk. Will ya?

All my friends have Greener Grass Syndromes.
We entertain pictures of ourselves "just grooving

with the hippies in natural mountain streams, naked and beautiful, splashing against the breasts of Mother Nature". I could go on—the chic cosmopolitan cafe society type, the creative businessman who's "dropped out" to a horse stud in the country. You name it, baby, I've had it. What about this one: a brilliant flautist/saxophonist, devoted to his craft, admired by the intelligentsia and the beautiful Bacardi people, and for kicks he gets it on with nuns. Or what about the rock-n-roll superstar, "doing what he wants, getting paid heaps for it and pulling in the chics". Don't laugh, it can happen to any filing clerk's assistant.

Sometimes, if you're lucky, you can begin to wander toward the greener grass. You think of some Heaven way over there, but once you reach it, you realize the new grass is still rooted in dirt.

A Photo of Myself in Heaven:
I used to see myself climbing coconut trees and dropping with those big brown nuts into thirty feet of tropical water . . . surrounded by laughing Polynesian ladies.

The Search:
When I was a child, my family lived in Melbourne, where peaches pop out of the dead winter trees and the grass under your feet manicures itself. My father

asked me one night if I wanted to live in Brisbane. I said "yeah, yeah" thinking of the coconut trees I'd climb, the coconut milk spilling over my face. When we touched down at Brisbane airport the sight of those corrugated-iron igloos, rising into the glare and haze, made me weep. Not a coconut tree in sight, no trees at all where I'd expected jungle. What a shithole. The coconut trees still existed though, they were just a bit further north—North Queensland, the Garden of Eden, the Promised Land. I bided my time.

Seven years later, with a pack on my back, I hitched to Cairns. If you ever find yourself in Cairns and you're down on the Esplanade, near the pier, look around for a coconut tree with foot notches carved into the trunk. I'm responsible for some of the higher ones. But ah, friends, how Fate had toyed with me!

There I was, crouched halfway up this tree, trying to hack new notches in the bark. This was IT, the realization of all my dreams. It was supposed to be fun, but it was bloody terrible trying to hang onto a tree and chop into it at the same time. And what made it worse was that down at the bottom of the tree was the most nagging devil you could ever have on your left shoulder. It was my mate, my Best Friend, the guy I'd hitched to Cairns with. He was "into ecology", an environmentalist, a conservationist, a bastard.

"You know what you're doing to that tree?"

"Shut up will ya!"

"You're killing it, you're cutting off its life blood."

"Shut up . . . Jesus!" When you're heading for Heaven, you can't be worried about a silly old tree.

"Incredible, I can't believe it. You're going to kill that tree just cause you want to climb up and knock down a few coconuts."

After about half an hour of that, coupled with fear of the police arriving, I came back down, back to Earth so to speak and I almost buried that bloody axe into his environmentally conscious brain.

I didn't find IT on the Cairns Esplanade, but I didn't give up.

We went to Holloway Beach, several kilometres from Cairns. At that time it was haven for about thirty hippies. This had to be IT—the land of honey and coconut milk. I stayed about half an hour.

The Search Ended:

At Holloway Beach I found *Nirvana*. Not that Heaven where happiness and fulfilment overflow with white-light ecstacy. No, not that Nirvana. This *Nirvana* was a stranded launch—home for millions of dry rot bacteria and eight anemic hippies. They had pneumonia but they were so aware they didn't know it. And *Nirvana* wasn't floating on the sea (which can be a symbol of Enlightenment); no, it was leaning to one side, rotting into the sand. Everybody was wet. When it rains up there, they call it The Wet. A lot of Sydney and Melbourne kids hadn't heard of it. As a creative gesture, someone had painted flowers and purple clouds on the hull of *Nirvana* and the picture was melting away in the constant downpour.

But that's not all! Beside the boat in the rain, a fire was somehow keeping itself alight, heating up (get this) a dozen frankfurts. That's what they were eating! And without tomato sauce! There's more. While the spiritual sailors sheltered aboard, the only girl I ever saw there (and I was expecting to see plenty with all-over tans) was tending to the frankfurts, handing them aboard. Chauvinists! That's right.

Later on I found out one of their staple meals was potato-chip sandwiches. Incredible tucker. Where have all the mangoes gone? And the pineapples and avocadoes and bananas and paw-paws and egg plants and coconuts? Where the hell were they? They were supposed to be dripping off the trees. All you have to do is reach out your arm, reach it out brother and taste the fruit of the Garden of Eden. Frankfurts and potato-chip sandwiches, just dripping off the trees.

So there I was, just standing on the sand watching another Utopia disintegrate like a soggy loaf of wholemeal bread.

Then this funny golliwog character bounced up to us. I swear he was skipping like a kangaroo. A hell man with excited eyes.

"Hi! How do you like our little community?"

"Really great. Beautiful." Yeah, I lied, but the Truth wasn't his scene.

"We got everything. There's a creek just at the back of the beach with ducks and birds and plenty of fish. We've got a canoe. [I looked at it. It must have had leprosy.] The fishing's great from the beach. You can build a shack up in the bushes there, help collect coconuts, do the rounds . . . "

"The rounds?"

"Yeah. We've got rounds. Like the cake and bread round, the vegetable round. A couple of days a week we visit different shops and bakeries. The people are really nice and give us what they can't sell."

It started to rain harder then, everybody scattered into old shacks and beaten-up trucks. I walked slowly through the trees and, taking a stand by the road, began hitching the thousand miles south, back to Brisbane.

Under the
Luscombe Bridge

One of Mucha's Ladies. A steel rod had been erected
through her body and, using it as a crutch, she
relaxed on it, her large breasts flowing one way, her
hips the other. And that rod, disguised among
nouveau art curves, had gone up to her head, behind
her eyes, making them hard and blank. She was
covered also in a flowing gown, soft as milk, the
edges swirling luxuriously. Looking out from the
picture, she gave you the big come on, come on into
my steel trap.

We were on the train to Beenleigh and Lisa's bag,
beside her on the seat, carried a print of that steely-
eyed damsel, glowering from the past. She watched
me the whole way as Lisa looked out of the window,
firm, serious as a nun on a Sunday outing.

The station was like a North Queensland town
where you step out of the train and the tropical heat
wraps a blanket round you. And stepping down into
that heat of summer-afternoon railway stations, you
take a step out of the air-conditioning into the past;
the old station tea rooms, the ticket office, the station
master's silver watch chain.

Lisa went to the Ladies leaving behind her lady bag; standing alone, this flowing lady, alone on the desert of the Beenleigh platform. I waited, thinking how often Lisa ducked off to the Ladies. She used to be quite concerned too, excusing herself with a "how embarrassing" and a pat on my arm. That was when I first knew her, over cups of black coffee and we'd have to interrupt an important philosophical climax with "how embarrassing". She asked me once, "Will you still love me when my bladder's gone?" It sounded like a Country and Western hit single. I crooned, "Yes My Darling You'll Still Be Mine", and in the background an Hawaiian guitar whined with beautiful melancholy.

Wood: for Puppets and Cellos
An old farmer waited on the platform, slightly bent and frail. I remember thinking his feet were made of wood with the leather of his riding boots just nailed on. He made small scuffing movements through the gravel as if each boot was pulled by a string. Lisa would think he was a "cute old fella". She likes little old men with husky voices. His eyes, worn and watery, were drawn to the steel-rod woman, as if he knew her from the old days, straining to see her across the desert platform. Perhaps it was she who held the strings to his boots.

Ballerina in the Rainbow:
We carried our camping things in a white bag and
the one with the Mucha lady, walking quietly
through town to the Rainbow Cafe. The sky was
overcast, ready to rain, clouds pushed down heavily
on the air pressuring the whole street into stillness.
Humidity.

We are familiar with the Rainbow Cafe, the old
Rainbow where we always eat two sausage rolls (for
Lisa) and an 'ot meat pie for me. I eat hot pies only
when I'm at the Rainbow. Not that Rainbow hot
pies are better than any others, it's just tradition.
And of course, tea. Lisa asks for the tea like this:

"Could we have a pot of tea please, with two
cups."

As if the waitress will bring silverware to our
laminex and meat pie table, and serve little chunks
of fruit cake, cut to convent parlour proportions.

We do not speak before the tea comes. Near us
is a glass cabinet displaying white cake decorations.
A ballerina, thin-legged, dances on the roof of a
white castle cake. A dead fly, black with death, lies
on its back at her feet. Another in the corner of the
cabinet, like a piece of discarded machinery.

The tea comes.

"Isn't this nice," she says, pouring with a straight
back; and I think, our setting should be an English
country garden, our furniture white and ornate, our
lawns green and wide.

Outside a soft summer rain begins to fall, moving
across like a spirit from the hills. We are not
prepared, only our toys fill the bags, books and

trinkets, the luggage of escaping children. The rain smells of wet summer inside the cafe. I look at the wall mirror beside our table. "Say Tristrams Please", greased over with the smoke from an endless line of hot pies reaching back to the time when Beenleigh men ate meat pies under the big fig tree.

Lisa sips her tea, her eyes squinting like a bushman with a pannikin. That same squint I'd see in Queen Street, on a paperseller's face as he leans down to adjust his bundles of news. That's how she drinks tea.

The tea-pot waits on the table, cheeky-spouted. The smell of rain.

The Bridge:

About twenty kilometres out of town, the Luscombe Bridge crosses a creek which later becomes the Albert River. It is still a child near the Luscombe Bridge having wandered along many miles out of the Lost World. I tell Lisa we could sleep under the bridge to keep dry and she says, "yes, I'd like that," as if I was asking her to a symphony orchestra concert, with cellos taken from green-felt cases. When she agrees I'm surprised. It seems unlike her to sleep under a bridge. I feel I should mention her convent manners, her superb tea-pouring abilities. But only Lisa could sleep under a bridge as if it were a four-poster.

The Cave:

The rain is still falling gently as we leave the car. Lisa thanks the driver, and soon we are alone, standing on the road in the slow rain, the smell of it steaming off the hot bitumen. In the distance clouds move around the crest of a hill, comforting the peak. It is warm rain, humid.

We climb down a stone wall and move in under the bridge. It is cosy and dry, like a different world, secure. Lisa says it is like a cave. Cars passing overhead seem miles away. Here I am with Lisa, safe under the bridge and just above us is a public thoroughfare where cars swish by on the wet road, windscreens foggy with conversation or silence which we cannot hear. Perhaps a lone driver, singing without inhibition, flat. We snuggle together like two moist frogs under the bitumen. It's a strange situation. Commuters, in their containers of steel and ourselves contained under the concrete of the bridge; like two eggs, separated by the membrane of the bridge, thinking of each other as stones, while less than a millimetre through the shell is a new life. My hand could move through the bitumen, and if I had ears on my fingertips, passing through the floor of the car, I could hear how it was inside their container. At least, for the split second they were above us. I could easily touch their feet, I could reach for their hand.

In a Bottle Garden:
The thud of water dripping on leaves echoes into our cave. Lisa takes some watermelon from the white bag and leaves it on the ground between us. Eating it I look out at the hill, the clouds moving swiftly up its slopes. I turn and Lisa is gazing down into the creek, calm-faced, and I notice again with a little surprise that her forehead is fairly large. She looks toward me with that large white forehead.

"Are we going for a swim?"

We move down into the trees, the leaves dripping onto our nakedness. A car shoots by overhead. Now only the sound of water running below. A king-fisher flashes past, blue-winged, dives away into the trees; I imagine his alert birdy eye watching from the shade. Stepping down the bank under the trees, darker now, moving around spider webs, wet tufts of grass. Silence, only the patter of rain on leaves. Glass beads of water hang ready to drop. A crow in the distance, if you listen for him. Our white bodies gleaming in the shade.

The water is clear to the rocks. We stand knee-deep, feeling it run between our legs. A fish dashes upstream, a whole school quickly behind. I look at her white bottom; she notices the desire in my face and smiles a little. We lower ourselves slowly, cringing at the genital region. The cold sharp water. Dropping under quickly, I flow into a silent universe, ever-exploding with silence, and emerge again, fresh. Little fish riding high above the sand float round the pillars of her legs.

Lisa goes back to the cave and I walk a little

upstream to sit down on a stone. The hill is still misty. Another car on the bridge, hissing water, gone. I am alone now. The world is moving very slowly, and on a wide front. I am nowhere to be seen. The crows over there flapping in the gum tree, lead useless lives. The rain has stopped. Even the crows are quiet for a moment. Ants are trailing busily between two unknowns. Only the sound of the stream like a thin glass rhythm tinkling quietly through a huge mass of white silence. A leaf, wet and dying ignores me. The trees move slowly in the breeze above the creek. I go back to Lisa.

The Hermetically-sealed Tin:
At night we roast potatoes in the coals, drink tea. The minister's daughter sipping from a tin pannikin, that's the turn-on. The lady bag is face down on the dirt floor now. We lie down to sleep. I put my hand on her bottom, kiss her ear, and now the little boy searching for milk and smooth stones wanders from my body and is gone among the trees.

Lisa is warm beside me.

Out across darkness, the hill rises blackly into the night. I look at the back of Lisa's head, leaning away from me; and, falling asleep, discover in the landscape of my head a tightly sealed tin with two little breasts, and on the inside, white smoky stuff.

For
Copernicus

In 2000 A.D. they discovered the earth was flat. Just
like a pancake. And Erhardt broke through the crust
and began falling down toward the light beneath
him. A joyous fall. He tumbled past the face of Cliff,
serene and soft, watching him fall. He tumbled on,
laughing and giggling, down towards the light
beneath him.

Council trams, buses, feet, briefcases bustled
together on the crust. No one even noticed the crack
Erhardt had fallen through. He fell on, down past
the water lilies, soft-spiking their sky with green-
cupped fingers. The light streamed upwards from
down beneath him. He laughed and chuckled and
fell on down towards it. He passed the roots of the
oak, long strong arms hugging the rocks and soil.
And still he fell, past the orange, the flower, delicate
and blue, down, past the big red apple till he left
the crust behind. He laughed and still he fell.

Dropping further into the light, he saw the crust
a long way off, turning over and over, rolling away
through space; now and then he could see the top

of it. Still it was the same—council trams, buses, feet, and briefcases. The light shone upwards around him and still he fell, like a laughing ball.

On Missing the
Twelve Apostles

For the purposes of this story, let's pretend I'm
sitting in Tamani's writing this. That's Tamani's,
Lygon Street, Carlton, where all the writers go. This
pretence is really quite pleasant; makes me feel
Parisien, writing great novels in smoky, coffee-
smelling cafes. *Les croissants et cetera.*

The story is one of adventure which could be
entitled "How I Hitched from Adelaide to Melbourne". But, it's not really adventure, because I
was picked up by George. George owns a 1972
Kombi, a Polaroid instamatic, Trouper (his pup),
cutlery and crockery for two, a wide mattress of
three-inch foam rubber covered with bright floral
cotton (tropical motif), a wet suit, a surfboard, a Bob
Marley haircut, a cheesy all-Australian grin, three
devices to make the van smell "real good", sagging
cheekbones, an inferiority complex, and a bag of
soap and things I left behind. The first words he
said to me when I hopped in were: I've just left me
girlfriend. It wasn't true. They'd split up about a
month before.

The only other thing about him is that he's "really havin' a great time, enjoyin' every minute of it. Bout two years it'll take me to go all the way round. Highway One."

Note that, Highway One!

George also owns a painting of Australia. It's on the side door of his van. There's a little blue line that leads across from about where Perth would be to about where Adelaide would be. I suppose that line is his replica of Highway One.

Do you begin to get the picture? Highway One. He had an obsession with it. Maybe he used to be a Jesus freak. What he wanted to do was just stay on that one road and follow it the "whole way round Australia". The concept is good. At the end, he'd have a thin blue line following the coastline, heading right back to Perth. But it's only a concept. He expected to have the ocean there, always at the corner of his eye. So there was his dream, "truckin' along the coast of Australia". And here I am sitting in Tamani's writing about it, breaking into bread rolls and watching the literary scene discussing "universal notions of prose".

Most of the time along the Adelaide-Melbourne stretch, you wouldn't know where the sea was, to left or right, not the remotest hint of water. But eventually we did sight the ocean welling up from the dry land, beautiful blue. George is right I thought. Why take a short cut to Melbourne (and save a mere eight hours) when sights like this are to be seen.

"Oooo shit!" That's what George said when he

saw the great blue vista.

Then he took a photo of it with his Polaroid. Othertimes, I had to take the photos. He gave me a short lecture on photographic aesthetics before he let me take the shots.

"Lot a people take pictures a sunsets and beaches but I doan reckon they're much good. They all look the same. I wanna have pictures of the road. There, now there's a good picture . . . "

His idea of a perfect photograph was a composition in which the road led straight on for about fifty metres and then turned to the left or right through some trees. It was always the same: "that's a beauty, get the camera ready when we come up to this one", and it would be the old faithful, a piece of road turning into some trees.

What a concept!

I drove for a while and he pulled out his *Holiday Guide to Australia* ($4.50 at Coles).

"There's some great things to see down along the Great Ocean Road, the Twelve Apostles, London Bridge."

His mouth watered as if he were talking about a bag full of lamingtons. Now for years I've wanted to see the Twelve Apostles (I had that type of upbringing) and now was my chance. He raved about it so much I thought he must have been Jesus disguised as a surfer.

Friends had told me about these huge stacks, standing magnificent, looking out to sea. Later, when he was driving, we suddenly sped past a small sign that said "Twelve Apostles", with an arrow pointing. I'm sure he saw it but he drove right past, intent on Highway One. Christ Almighty! I couldn't speak. And it's not part of the hitch-hiker's role to start telling the driver where to go. I just sat, looking into the rear-view mirror, trying to glimpse them. I felt like a piece of stone.

Two apostle heads appeared above the cliffs, and they really were grand and sacred, vestments of earth colours, heads held high. Jesus was there of course, but, like the sea, so far out and all-embracing, so obvious; not at all extraordinary.

And here I am at Tamani's writing about George and wishing there was some way my imagination could bring the sea into this tight little cafe.

The First
Unreasonable Laughter

If we were gods (and which one of us isn't), we could have looked down on a certain island (now called Australia) while it was still very innocent, while the eucalypts were new in their evolution along the east coast. The Eucalyptus Period, just begun, and under the bark of those millions of trunks, an absolute wood purity that only an axe could find.

Axes found it of course. But before that (while Australia was coming into its seventh youth) the first Laughing Bird was born from eucalyptus wood.

Later, we came with axes.

The gods of ourselves were listening as the first chock of the axe echoed through the silent forests. And, Heaven help us, we tried to find those gods by breaking into the sacred gums and by axing into the throat of the Laughing Bird to discover its secret of happiness. And we found there, among the pink organs of its throat, something we should never have seen.

The Fling
Contract

Fling: Spell of indulgence in impulse, (to have one's
——); that type of sexual relationship in which the
heart is sealed with lead and the animal of passion
rages freely throughout the land.

Contract: Enter into business or legal engagement.
Every fling should have one.

One of the tyres has just gone on us. We're nowhere,
in the dark in far western Queensland, semi-desert
country. We pull off the road, switch off. Rob swears
quietly. There's no spare, we can't do a thing but
enjoy the dark and the quiet, the pure air. Not a
light anywhere except stars. Kay and I look out the
window. It feels like we've been crawling along the
bottom of a sea, stars floating way up on the surface.

Rob and I climb into the back of the van and bed
down on the mattress. Kay tucks into her sleeping
bag up front. It's quiet as we snuggle into our

blankets. As I close my eyes I have an image of Kay cooking eggs that morning for breakfast. I'm a chauvinist at heart, really turned on by women who look content while they're frying eggs. I remember how I wanted to kiss her then. A short gentle paternal kiss, a kiss over the scrambled eggs. Another image of her comes to me. She is naked beside the river where we washed ourselves, her body like a white hand holding the dark dainty flower of her vagina. I picture us waist deep in water and all I desire is to kiss her right eye, just as it closes, with the other eye still open, watching me. That's innocent enough.

At night, Rob is like a refrigerator—usually quiet, but sometimes getting noisy for no apparent reason. I've been on my back now for quite some time, looking at the roof of the Kombi. Kay is rustling in the front seat. I have my attention on her.

Whispering.

"Are you awake?"

"Yes." She slides out of the bag a little. "Look at those lights out there. And the throbbing, can you hear that?"

I lean into the front seat. Through the dark eucalypts, blue-green lights twinkle. A machine is turning over.

"Rob'd say that was a UFO." She whispered it, so as not to wake him.

"Yeah, he's like that . . . he can believe in anything."

I'm glad she wants to talk. My chest is pressing

hard against the seat. I'm thinking about kissing her by holding her face with one hand and slowly moving my lips toward her mouth. That makes my heart beat faster.

"I can hear your heart beating."

"Yeah?" attempting to be casual, "is it that loud?"

"Can't you turn it down?"

She laughs at her own joke, looking at me. Her eyes are shining, her lips too. Now listen: At times, we force our bodies to do things, say things. It's a leap into the dark, we don't know how we'll land. I let my hand take that leap. In slow motion, it travels toward her head. I clear out, let that hand go, watch it from a distance. It lands on her head fairly well, considering, rather gently. It begins to move her head toward me, way up in the dark where I'm waiting. Then it hits a rough spot, the head won't come.

"Go on, go back to bed," says her pretty head.

"Okay."

I slither back into the hole of my blanket and collapse from exhaustion. Rob hasn't stirred. There is silence except for the machine down through the trees.

"What do you think it is?" she says.

"What? . . . those lights?"

"Yeah . . . I suppose we'll see in the morning."

"In the morning, the machine won't matter. Once daylight comes, everything changes."

That was a dramatic observation. "Once daylight comes everything changes." I let the drama of it sink through the silence.

A bit of a snuffle from Rob.

"Could you really hear my heart before?" I ask.

"Yes. Were you scared of the machine?"

"No. I was scared though."

"Why?"

"Because I was going to kiss you."

Silence. Only the throbbing of the machine, through the trees.

"You've made it hard for me."

"Why?"

Rob made waking-up noises. We remained silent for a while till he settled.

"Another relationship . . . I can't handle it."

"Forget about it then."

"It's funny. I've had so much attention lately . . . I can't do anything with you."

"Okay. Good."

She held her hand toward me. I reached to hold it. It was an uncomfortable stretch but worth it.

"I'd like to."

"What? Do something with me?"

"Yeah, maybe. It's over with Tim now you know. I need something permanent. I want to sink into somebody. I've made a decision about it really. There's something with Bernie and I. He cares for me."

"Good."

"But you . . . "

"I only want a fling."

"I wouldn't mind but . . . "

"No, no. People really do need something permanent. I've got that. It's good. It's the end of that lonely sinking feeling . . . I'm just after a bit of sexual excitement."

"I know just the girl, I'll introduce you."

"No, come on."

"You'd like her."

"No, let's just go to sleep. Forget about it. It'd be good for you and Bernie. I like him."

"I'm sorry."

"It's okay. Feel free to come over and rape me anytime you like."

"Look, there's something down near the machine."

"What?"

"More lights, moving."

I leaned over to see. I brushed her cheek, by accident, a mutually agreed upon accident. Then, of course, it happened. The flames of passion etc. We kissed, she sank down into the seat, I leaned down over her like a thick black snake hanging off a tree. Her mouth seemed to swallow my head. That was okay but I didn't want her getting anywhere near my heart and I could feel that beginning to slip into her dark mouth.

Sexual contact melts inhibitions, creates bonds. I didn't want that. Every kiss forms another link in a chain of complication, a chain that rusts into the flesh.

We talked again. She showed me a movie about herself. I was the only person in the cinema, in this Kombi, in the middle of the desert.

Part One—entitled "How I Lost My Virginity" —begins with herself introducing the film as a kind of hostess. She wears a gown of dark blue water. Her blond hair floats through the water and in the depths are glimpses of her white body. After this introduction, the movie starts at a country dance, she is "a sexy young thing". She walks into the hall, bodgies one side, girls the other. A combo plays a sick Bill Haley style as she takes the floor with a greasy lad wearing sweat thickened stove-pipe jeans. He's a bad dancer. He takes her outside, does it quick, hurts her. She returns to the hall dishevelled, a spot of blood coming through her dress, blood in the recesses of her green eye.

Before the next scene, she appears again in her water gown, smiling, the perfect hostess. You can see she's happy to be a star in her own movie. She introduces Part Two, "How I Took Life with Both Hands Hoping to Bring Sensitivity to My Soul". She enters from stage left wearing a sandpaper suit. Underneath the sandpaper she's made of steel, right through. Her face is clear, uplifted. A man with long blond hair enters from stage right offering a mushroom. He gives it to her. She eats it and her face turns to stone. He opens his jeans, holds out an erect penis. She opens her abrasive legs. He inserts the penis. They move back and forth. Blood drips from her vagina, he collapses castrated. She hoses the blood away.

Two men enter, one immediately behind her, the other from stage right. Both have erect penises. They are holding them. They enter her very quickly, the sandpaper suit falls away, the steel was never there, her flesh bleeds onto the white skin.

She enters in her water gown, bowing effusively, her hands joined, tucked down between her legs, smiling. She remains so, bent over, slumped.

The end. A good movie.

Rob hasn't stirred.

"What about the two men, who were they?"

"I thought I could handle that sort of thing, but I couldn't."

"What, two partners?"

"Yeah."

Such a pretty face! A chauvinist like me doesn't expect that a pretty face masks thoughts of group sex.

"What about the hippie guy. Why did you do that to him?"

"I didn't mean to hurt him. It just happened. It must have been the stone."

I lean into the front seat, try to encircle her with my arms. She pulls her face away. I've forgotten what she really looks like. I pull her closer. We move into each other's mouths.

She pushes me away. "Could you fall in love with me for just a week?"

"What, a week-long contract?"

"Yeah. Set ourselves up in a motel in Surfer's, drink gin and martinis, lie in bed for three days . . ."

"A week . . . !"

". . . and put me in a love coma." She moves closer.

"Go down to the bar at four every afternoon, hang off the stools drinking Brandy Alexanders."

"Pick up some supple-bodied hedonists for a bit of group stuff."

"What about it?"

"Maybe I am too young to settle down."

"Yeah, maybe . . ."

HEAVEN AND HELL
IN
YOUR OWN HOME

Buddha and the Seven Dwarfs

A common Zen saying:

> Those who know do not speak;
> Those who speak do not know.

So don't bother with this story, just sit there and be, or perhaps you could contemplate a Zen koan: What is the sound of one hand clapping?

The monk who made up that question (his name was Hakuin) was a contemporary of Bonnie Prince Charles, the Great Pretender. Do you get the symbolism of that? In the East a monk leading searchers toward Enlightenment; in the West, a Bonnie Prince trying to snatch the power of the English monarchy. Kipling said "the twain" would never meet. But at our place, we were visited by some Great Pretending Buddhists who'd give the lie to that.

The koan for this story is: How did Snow White dispose of the Seven Dwarfs after Prince Charming awakened her?

For our household, it was necessary to contemplate this ridiculous question in the hope that we'd learn something from the fable. For Snow White, of course, it all ended "happily ever after" and for the sake of your own innocence, I ask you not to pursue the "hows" and "how comes" of that tale. We had to because, boys and girls, we were beset by the seven evil Zen Bludgers.

Terry invited them home. They were standing in the rain in King George Square just "being". He "be-ed" with them for a few hours then asked them home for a meal. He did "the decent thing"; after all, it was just a few days before Christmas.

I won't describe them all. It's not necessary to describe individuals whose only concern is fusion with the One. But for those who aren't into Zen, I'll give you the details on two of them. If you're Enlightened and know that all is the One anyway, just skip a few paragraphs. But before you go, answer this koan: Why read my unenlightened scriptures? You should be in the garden just "blissing out", or laughing at super-jokes no one else can see, or listening to rock-n-roll with detached admiration while drinking Coke with some kind of Coke-proof Zen stomach lining.

Anyway, for the others:

There was Doc—please pronounce it Dark. Yeah that's right man, he was a beautiful golden boy from California, a dwarf version of Ed Sullivan and he made Jackie Gleeson look thin (canned Zen laughter).

"Man, have you ever looked at anyone's face for long enough to really see it? S'beautiful man. I mean . . . I mean, just your own face in the mirror. Wow, you can see a map of the land."

That was his trip, looking into his own face. That's cool with me. But when I wake up in the morning, when I walk into my own lounge room, first thing, I don't want to see it. With an empty stomach, I don't want to see a Californian Reclining Buddha staring into a mirror, surrounded by lotus-posturers. I don't want that to happen to me before I get my Corn Flakes down.

Dopey—an elongated dwarf. His eyes were huge and blue, his head shone, the rest of his body hung off that like a piece of rag. He had that starved, health-food look. He didn't talk much. None of them did, they just laughed and smiled insanely.

The important thing is, they didn't have Snow White or the Buddha with them.

And I wondered how the hell she got rid of them.

The Dignities:
In Buddhism there are four dignities: walking, standing, sitting, lying. To hold any of these postures is to perform a beautiful act, a ritual.

The Dwarfs concentrated on sitting. They did it very well. They did it all day for two days round our kitchen table. We couldn't get in there to eat. Terry sat with them. I noticed he started laughing in a similar way, jiggling up and down on his stomach, laughing low down like a Buddha, instead of his usual high-up-scrawny-neck laugh. He wouldn't cook anymore either.

"It's the Boodhist way, unless food is offered to us, we can't eat," said Dark.

And neither could we. It was easier to starve than cook for seven philosophers who'd formed a phalanx round your kitchen table, eternally ready for the Tea Ceremony. No matter where you were in the house you could hear them talking and laughing, you could hear their fat ear lobes rattling the way the Buddha's must have.

The Important Concept of Being:
This isn't the usual concept of Being as used in most schools of Buddhistic thought. This is the concept of Being Zapped. It goes like this. If you feel you should be somewhere, and the "feel" is right, you will be taken there magically. So if you want to travel cheaply, become a member of The Zapping Buddhists Travel Club. Dark told us he was once zapped to Scotland. That stuck in my mind . . . Scotland! What a place to be zapped to. Why not Nepal, Calcutta, Tokyo even. Scotland was too straight, too conservative. I tried to imagine what a Buddhist would do in Scotland. All I knew was that they played soccer there and maybe they had moors. A Californian Buddha like him just didn't fit in. But then I had this vision . . .

The Glass Grandstand Vision:

I was in the shower; you know how thoughts and images pour in while you're showering. It suddenly struck me that Scotland must have a Glass Grandstand. And this grandstand was the only place in Scotland which could tolerate Dark. Why? Because if you looked up through this grandstand you came to the overwhelming conclusion that thousands of Scots were giving you the arse.

The fantasy carried me a bit further. I certainly enjoyed the thought of Dark having to sleep under such a load of negative vibes. These are the types of places one gets zapped to.

I went on, encouraged by the warm water, and imagined the crowd were listening to a man with a faint but penetrating voice. He didn't shout or enthuse, but he was heard. He was loved. In the words of the popular song celebrating him,

> He was an ex-rock-n-roll star,
> He'd taken all the strings off his guitar.

To speak simply, he was charming. I felt he was some kind of hero who could be a personal saviour for everyone. My daydreams under a warm shower often give me glimpses of the heroes I need and desire. But just glimpses.

Zen and the Concept of No-Food:

Having had that vision, I thought I'd slip in and eat before the phalanx blocked up the kitchen with good vibes. I knew they'd soon be sitting round the table like a macabre but dull surprise party. Food stocks were low, and maybe once they were finished, the Dwarfs would "feel" it was time to go. Hi ho, hi ho. I met Leo in the kitchen, he had the same idea.

"Any Corn Flakes mate?"

"No, I've just finished them, sorry."

"As long as they're finished mate, as long as they're finished."

We exchanged knowing glances.

I ate six oranges that morning; Leo started spooning down sugar and jam. We got stuck into the healthy food too, the things they liked, raw cabbage, carrots, everything—all eaten quietly. We drank the last of the milk, though I was worried they'd find the powdered stuff in the cupboard— and they did.

Rule 431 B:

We left the kitchen with blissful grins on our faces, passed the Buddhists in the lounge (Dark staring at his image in a mirror) and retired to my room to plot. The sausages and chops waited in the fridge, protected because Buddhists are vegetarian. We planned a nice meal for later on. We were wrong: one should always live in the present.

Buddhists are vegetarian but then Rule 431 B overrules the vegetarian diet. Rule 431 B states that the Buddhist must eat all that is offered to him. So there you are. Those bastards ate our sausages and

laughed while we sat in the bedroom trying to digest
Corn Flakes and jam and raw cabbage.

Zen and the Art of "Feel":
This is important, especially to "hung-up city
freaks" like us, because the "feel" replaces the
"think". For instance, they felt it was okay to
ritually sit round our kitchen table for a couple more
days, while we felt crapped off with them. But it
was different you know, our feel was negative. They
were relieving us of negative "feels", bringing them
out of us. Their positive was attracting our negative.
We should have been grateful, they were sucking
up our bad "feels" like a spiritual vacuum-cleaner.
    "Hey man has there ever been a Black Witch
living in this house?"
    "No, nothing like that here, we don't like that
sort of thing."
    "What I mean is, you ever practice black magic
round here?"
    "No, not us."
    "The vibes here man, are so heavy, frightening
. . . it's like the whole street is turned in on itself,
under some incredible power. I can feel it."
    "No, not our street."
    "Tell ya bout this dream I had last night. I was
lookin in my mirror you know, and suddenly I saw
it, a toad, really staring hard back at me. Was big
too, big as me. Then it got all black, and white spew
come out of its mouth, and it changed into a witch,

a Black Witch, all painted up, trying to look nice. Freaky."

"No, never seen her round here."

Zen and the Art of Telling People to Piss-off:
The plots:
  (a) Offer them poisoned apples.
  (b) Ask them to go.
  (c) Invite the band round for a twenty-four-hour jam. But dwarfs only know one song, and the toad-heads would probably want to sing along. One of them had a one-string guitar. "I'm headin to Unity man, always One."
  (d) I'd lead them off, "feeling" the way, following a vision of a Glass Grandstand in Scotland, lose them somehow and return surreptitiously to enter the house by a secret hatch.

Plotting made us hungry. I've noticed that about food. If you eat healthy food, like apples, raw carrots and cabbage, orange juice etc., before long you're hungry as hell for things like toasted Spicy Fruit Loaf, sausages, chips, and chocolate. Leo and I went up the shop and bought two pieces of fish in breadcrumbs, a sav in batter, five olives, a pickled onion, twenty cents worth of chips, six sea scallops, a block of chocolate, two caramel malted to take away, and seven big rosy red apples.

Haiku for Christmas:
At school we performed a Christian play. Two men who'd stolen money wanted to go somewhere secret to count it out.

First thief: "Lets go up this dark alleyway and count it out."

Second Thief: "God can see us there."

And so it went . . . "into that bush" . . . "no, God can see us there" . . . "down this old coal mine" . . . "no, God can see us there."

I forget how it ended. The money probably rotted in their hands, just like our fish and chips. We couldn't go home. We went down a side street to the riverbank. I knew the Buddha could see us there eating chocolate, fish and chips, and malteds, but I was feeling the pangs of self-pity as it started to rain on us. We moved in under a tree like a couple of old drunks who'd been wandering Buddhists in their youth. What a way to spend the day before Christmas.

"Those bastards have probably got thousands stacked away somewhere, in case this doesn't come off."

"Yeah, rich parents, saving up their dole cheques for them."

"Christmas Eve
Rain falls softly on
Chocolate wrapper—
Wet fish and chips."

"What's that?"

"Haiku, it's Zen poetry man, captures a sad fleeting mood. But you can only use seventeen syllables."

Leo counted them on his fingers. "Yeah, gee, I might do one . . . um . . .

Christmas Eve
Snow White loses
Virginity
To Seven Dwarfs."

"Not sad enough."

On the way home, we passed the shop and saw one of the Dwarfs buying chocolate frogs. We would have leapt on him if we weren't so embarrassed.

"What about this one?

Chocolate frog
Sits serene, unwrapped
Pushing Buddhist down
Its gullet."

We took the apples home but didn't have time to inject them with ratsack.

"Wow man, beautiful apples."

Zen and the Art of Photograph-taking:
Leo and I snuck back to my room. We reviewed the schemes. In the kitchen we heard the bliss freaks talking heavy with Terry. Maybe he'd go with them.

"I hope he doesn't. His mother'll blame me if he does."

"Don't worry mate, he likes eating too much."

"Yeah, but he likes Buddhism, he invited them back here. I have to admire him sometimes. He leads a simple life."

"Yeah, he is a bit bloody simple."

Soon Terry came into the room and started photographing us. We sat there slumped against the wall just looking at him, wondering whether he'd follow the Buddhists or not. He swayed this way and that, squashed himself into corners to get the right shots. He seemed fairly pleased with himself. He still had the lense cap on.

"Just got me camera back. They didn't fix it properly."

"Is it loaded?"

"Yeah but it doesn't work."

"Well stop taking photos, they're pricey to develop."

"Won't develop em. I'll just throw the film away."

"Wow man, that's beautiful yer know, that's Zen man. I mean you've let go man, you're free. You know you can't catch the Now in that little black box. You've got it all inside your head man, you're free," I said.

Then he sprung it on us. "I told the Buddhists to go."

Leo and I nearly brought our chips up.

"Wad they say?"

"They said they didn't mind . . . but they changed a bit."

"How did they change?"

"They just didn't talk to me so much."

"It seems pretty bad to chuck em out, it's raining, Christmas eve too."

"Yeah, but that's their way of life. Christmas means nothing to them. And they're boring me mate. They're like those Jehovah's Witnesses who came, they never let up."

"True. Where are they going?"

"Back to King George Square. They can sleep there tonight . . . in under the Reserve Bank."

Terry is the only person I know who can get out of doing the dishes just by saying, "I don't feel like it mate." He says it with such conviction that you have to walk away shrugging your shoulders and do it yourself. They left him a note.

Terry,
> thanks very much for being honest with us and telling us to go. You are free now of negative feels. The others still have them inside. We stayed to absorb the power of the Black Witch I dreamt about. Our life is only meant to help others,
>> Bliss

They all signed it. They were gone, out into the rain.

Leo and I felt a bit uneasy.

The Paint Man

He stands high on the ladder, like one on stilts, faraway. Perhaps his face is painted white, clown-like. Is he smile/sad or something else? The children wonder at the Paint Man, high up near the ceiling. He is too tall for the room. His neck is bent at the ceiling.

The children giggle behind the door, peek out. "You go in."

"No, no, you first."

The Paint Man sees their heads around the door, pulls a face. The little girls laugh and struggle with each other to run from the doorway. Soon, they're watching him again. Up the legs of the ladder, across the overalls, brightly speckled, the face. Ah! The Paint Man! Run!

They hold a golliwog through the door. It wobbles like a crazy wild-eyed Black Man. The Paint Man sees it. He looks frightened, nearly topples over backwards off the long wooden legs. The girls giggle and jump with glee. Their dresses fly up. The Paint Man watches.

"Don't dare touch us Paint Man."
"Don't put paint on our faces."
"Do you want to paint our tongues?"
They push them out and let them fly back in, foop, like elastic. They tease the Paint Man, coyly daring him, their hands tucked down between their legs. He dips the paint brush into the tin, uncrooks his neck from watching them, brushes a few slow measured strokes across the ceiling.
The girls are giggling in the hallway outside the door. He hears their feet thumping.
"You go dancing in like this. Put this lady's bag on first and hold the ruler up high. I'll sing."
Giggles. Their concert is four seconds long. She enters like a miniature stripper, cat walker, hips swaggering. She eyes the Paint Man's face, high up on the ceiling. Then suddenly, an exit, full of squeals and laughter.
The Paint Man brushes slowly.

They hold a doll through the door.
"By the legs, hold it by the legs, don't let the Paint Man see you."
He roars from the ceiling. They run madly down

the corridor, out of earshot. He looks slowly, awkwardly toward the ceiling.

"That was a rude doll. It's got no clothes."
Paint Man: "Yes."
"Were you scared when you saw it from behind the door?"
Paint Man: "Yes."
"I bet I can scare you again . . . . Are you going to paint my head white and pull it off?"

"You're not allowed to do that."
Paint Man: "What?"
"Um . . . you're not allowed up the ladder, it's too high. Your face looks awful up there."

"Throw this water over the Paint Man."
Giggles out in the hallway. He sees the edge of one of their dresses. Peeking round the door. She pokes her tongue out at him, then laughs.

The little girls are watching him through the window. He sees them laughing but he can't hear it. He leans over to the window, opens his huge mouth, growls, his hot breath fogging the glass. The girls run away.

"You're not allowed to do that," she yells.

"Lets push over the Paint Man's ladder."
   "No he'll fall."
   "He won't."
   "Emily, don't be silly."
   "You're silly."

The Paint Man is down, like a performer whose stilts have broken. He doesn't know how to act at this level. He moves quicker, jerkily. His neck is still at an angle; tough brown skin at the back of his neck.
   She runs out of the room screaming.

Inside the room, in the corner is a naked doll's leg. Emily stands stock still in the other corner screaming. She discharges into her pants.
   Paint Man: "Come here, take off your pants."

The Paint Man struggles on the floor, his head still to one side; the tough skin at the back of his neck.

Emily's doll is smeared with white paint. The ceiling is only half-painted. The Paint Man's ladder is broken. White paint, flowing from the overturned tin, insinuates itself through the doll's hair.

Descent after Midnight

This story is completely REAL. No conjuring or colouring of facts here, no characterization, nothing but Real Life. Let's see if you find it interesting.

What Is That Reality Known as Stairs?
Our house has two storeys (top and bottom). To get to the lower level, you pass through a door that looks like any other door on the top storey but, once opened, there before you a steep staircase leads down and turns a mysterious corner. It makes you think, you know; it makes you wonder as you step down, if you're just descending one floor of a perfectly normal disintegrating suburban house, or if you're descending. Descending in some archetypal manner, changing levels you know, moving into a new plane.

Them:

The couple that live below are lovely. How else can I say it, they gave us coloured pencils and elephants for Christmas. We hear them laughing together down below and smell their incense as it rises up the staircase into our rooms. I know a lot about them; things you wouldn't be interested in; but maybe this will catch your eye. We know they have long showers (probably together) because the hot water system is upstairs, and sitting round the kitchen table drinking tea, we hear it burning, and look at each other over cups of char, and think of them down there in the shower.

(But this is Real Life so I have to admit what one of us once said: "They're using an awful lot of gas." This is the type of comment that makes life Real. An unkind comment upstairs, while below, a quaint couple splash together under the shower.)

A Yellow Moment with Leo:

Anyway, late the other night we'd all dispersed to our separate rooms. They'd gone down through that doorway which looks so ordinary, down past the corner in the staircase. I was still in the lounge with Leo talking like this:

Leo: "I'm entering a yellow phase at the moment."

Me: "Oh. Yeah yeah." I think I knew what he meant.

Leo: "I'm going to buy a yellow t-shirt and yellow

shorts and yellow boots and then I'm going to get tanned up."

Me: "Yeah?!" He's a weird man, but innocent.

Leo: "Yeah, but that's not all, it's a yellow spiritual time, a spinning flying yellow, not a Gaugin . . ."

At this point the ordinary staircase door opened. He was there (I needn't mention his name) and he said:

"Come and have a look at this fantastic light show."

A Sensational Household Custom:
Before we descended I thought about a household custom. One person mans a light switch and turns it on and off quickly to imitate the strobe effect. Meanwhile, someone else grooves round trying to look sensational. I thought it might be something in that vein, but no.

The Lift:
We all went down the stairs and turned the corner, the six of us, coming out of our bedrooms. It was very late at night. He led us into the dark rooms below, pitch black, and finally into the small high bedroom where she could be vaguely made out lying across the bed. If I was to exaggerate, I'd say their bedroom was similar to a lift well, very high, and

we were standing in the dark at the bottom, like a crowd in a lift.

"Look up there."

We did. On the ceiling were groups of fire flies, flashing their lights, occasionally moving about. They appeared to be miles up. Nobody was upstairs now, we were all crammed into the lift, looking up, getting kinks in our necks. I sat on the bed and watched. The fire flies were like stars in the ceiling of their bedroom. A planetarium.

Then a slight jolt told me we were moving up the lift well. Passing steadily through the darkness of the upper rooms, we left the house and moved out into the sky. The fireflies came with us of course and rested in our eyes and hearts. I looked back to see sheets of roofing turning end on end after the slow explosion of our exit. We moved higher above the rooftops, the others still looking up and Leo, with a yellow smile glowing out of his face, leaned over and whispered to me.

"If eyes are not licked they turn bad, they rot like mangoes." Then he held his arms high above his head and, in a last rush, we were all assumed into the sky.

It's the next morning now. Everyone else is still asleep. There's no sound in the street, or in the house, no gas burning in the hot water system. The early sun is on a mango tree, a summer storm cloud passes slowly by the kitchen window, and down in the yard a bird sitting for a long time on a branch opens and closes its beak, without making any sound.

The roof is okay.

Family
Responsibilities

My sister, the Monkey, we used to call her, died a few weeks before the rest of us. We sent her body to the Black Man (who hammered her into a shallow bowl) and waited for my brother to die.

His body was flatter, like a saucer. The Black Man used rivets to join it to Monkey's body. A snug fit.

My mother and father followed each other quickly. I hardly remember who went first.

I was the last to go, but by the time the Black Man was pulling my arms and legs off, there was quite a nice sphere being formed. He had to work nights but even under this constant pressure, he never tired. Such a wonderful craftsman he was, there was no indication his materials had come from the meat of our family.

My own contribution he'd obviously planned well in advance. My head, he dropped inside the sphere through a small chink which he covered by meticulously working and re-working the basic material of my right arm.

Child's
Play

My mother who was always a dramatic person woke me one morning with this:

"Of course you know the children have gone wild!"

It was the "of course" that sent me into a spinny. If something's really amiss, mother always says "of course". This morning there weren't the usual reproaches in her voice.

1. "Fancy not being up at this hour."
2. "You haven't read a paper for weeks."
3. "You don't know what's happening in the world."

But who cares what's happening in the world. It's heading for wrack and ruin. What more do we have to know? Why depress ourselves again every morning by reading the paper?

And she thinks I'm lazy, thirty years old next month and I still haven't started my career. She dreams of the day I'll go off to work with contracts and other executive trappings in my little briefcase.

Anyway what children? What children have gone

wild? Surely not my own. Doris had left mother and I years back and she wasn't the type to let the children have a decent spit. Then there were the neighbourhood kids, they weren't too bad, noisy and unmannered, but that's kids. Some would help me at times with the vegetable garden.

"What children?" I said.

"The whole city. It's school holidays you know and the kids have gone beserk, smashing everything. There's too many for the police."

"Dear," I said but I couldn't really care.

"Now come on, get up. You know I need you today. Agnes is being buried. You've got to pick up Floss and Bert in half an hour and then the two Bourke sisters. God help them—I hope there's no kids smashing up their place."

Another day, another burial. My mother attracts funerals like flies. The house brims over with powdered aunts and sponge cream cakes, sandwiches without crusts—all the funeral trappings. With all the training I've had I'd be an undertaker myself except for the black gloves.

The aunts are in the lounge room now with powdered jowls, the tears are over. Agnes has been put down, so to speak. With dainty cake forks, the aunts are popping pieces of sponge into their mouths. I like to see a nice tea party, with silverware. Mother does it so well. But enough's enough. I have to get out, escape to my vegie garden. The tomato bushes look marvellous.

My mind is wandering among the carrots and capsicums when, quite suddenly, I become aware that there's a gang of children holding pieces of piping and wooden stakes coming through the fence toward me. I recognize Shane and Cyril, my favourites, and some of the others but today there seems to be a tough element as well. They look serious and determined. I begin to realize what's happening . . .

There's about twenty of them, like a tribe of Vikings, a primitive army of boys and girls. Seeing me, they leap the fence without hesitation. Am I to be a victim to their rusty pieces of steel? Shane stops them and speaks for me. I'm surprised at how much he understands for a boy of his age. He's quite sensitive. Begrudgingly, they allow me to return to the house but some of the little buggers poke me in the back as I make my way through. The sun is on their hard angry faces. Men's faces on children's bodies. They're squinting in the sun. Hoary-headed kids. Dwarfs. God I can't stand dwarfs. Or kids. I lock the back door and hear their leader giving orders with unquestionable authority. They obey and set about stoning the mansion next door. The Jamieson's house. I can't do anything to stop them but mother never liked the Jamieson's very much anyway.

The aunts and relations are watching the riots on television. The city centre is packed with children, "like swarming ants, relentlessly destroying everything in their path", says the TV commentator.

I'm scared. We all are. I look out the window where the children are still working at the Jamieson mansion. There's so many of them. Some are well-dressed—girls in floral shorts, boys with little blue waistcoats and neat Italian leather shoes, covered in dust from the constant pounding. There's one of those thick-limbed tough girls, very butch. Just like Sylvannia who used to pick on me at school. She's bossing the younger boys around. Bitch.

They've developed an elaborate way of throwing stones—all trained up like machines. They swing their arms (about three times) turn to face the building, turn away from the building and eventually throw the stones backwards over their heads. They keep the rhythm with a song that carries along in a restrained monotone, suddenly breaking out in a roar as the stones are hurled. The projectiles are thrown so they all come down together. Leading the chanting is an elegantly dressed girl. Her navy blue pinafore looks neat and pressed. The children watch her to stay in rhythm; she commands obedience just by her manner. Obviously, she was the best behaved girl in the class, now turned rebel; righteousness is with her. I find myself almost admiring her, then glimpsing just the side of her face, I'm thrown into confusion. My God, it's Rosemary Towner, from grade three! But it can't be, not the same girl who sat next to me at the convent, who teased and ignored me, hated me, while I thought she was the prettiest thing. If only I could get a clear glimpse of her.

Mother calls me away from the window to attend to one of the aunts. Everyone in our house is afraid.

Outside the singing rises and falls but continues like a menacing wind. The TV reports their activities elsewhere in the city, filming the packs of little wretches as they tear the clothes off middle-aged frightened people. The noise of a tremendous upheaval from the adjoining yard diverts our attention from the screen. Mr. Jamieson is running from the side door near the kitchen. They climb onto his back and begin clawing his face. Others are tearing off his shirt and biting into his skin. He sees me watching helpless from our window, but his eyes are those of a dead man, blank.

"The axe! The axe!" he yells.

He was trying to make it to the toolshed where he kept his only weapon. His carcass now lies like a large grub on the lawn. He used to be so proud of that lawn. The little beasts are screaming with delight, running round him like ants. Some of them are inside his house now. Our turn must be next.

Rosemary is nowhere in sight. She must have gone in with the others.

Sister Bourke nags me till I check on all the doors. It's useless but I go about it to please her. At the back near the laundry, I notice the bolt of the lock is not working. I try to put it in place and realize with horror the whole door is off its hinges. As it topples toward me, I see on the other side, a boy and the girl who looks like Rosemary, clinging to the door like two moist slugs, consuming it into their bodies. Pulling the door open I find the boy is an old school acquaintance, looking exactly as he did in Grade Eight. I didn't like him then—he was so snobby—but I was pleased to see him now. He wasn't one day older.   "Davies. Phil Davies! What are you doing here? You haven't aged . . . You marvellous boy!" I had to lay it on a bit. Maybe he could save us.

"Some people can jump the gap," he said with this strange arrogant sort of smile and turned, sharing a private joke with the girl who kept her face always away from me.

It seemed ridiculous to be standing there talking about school days while the neighbours were being murdered. I was trying to entertain him and at the same time keep an ear cocked to the dining room in case Davies was just a decoy. He knew what I was thinking so he could afford to be casual. He didn't introduce the girl who said nothing. Phil could sense I was curious to see her but he stood between us and maintained polite conversation.

"What do you get out of all this, Phil?" I asked lightly as if my fate had no part in the destruction which had reached a new climax next door.

He told me he was doing it "just for fun" and kept smiling. At this the girl seemed to laugh in a familiar kind of way—reminding me of someone so close, like a deja-vu laugh.

The Great
White Forest

Sometimes you can think you're in a movie. It
doesn't take too much—new shoes, new pose, new
room, and suddenly the space around you is special,
exciting, anything could happen. It was like that
when I moved from Queensland into an upstairs
room in Carlton. There I was, a fine figure, ready
to create a new image of myself, to see how the other
half lived.

The room had a fireplace, a front window looking
out to a Jewish funeral parlour, and a double bed.
It was the double bed that gave a poor lonely
Queensland boy his ideas.

On the Colour of Rain: For a while, nothing
happened, the movie froze in scene one, with myself
looking quietly through the lace curtains out into
the strange Melbourne-coloured rain. Grey.
Queensland rain had always been silver or red, like
glass hibiscus falling into the garden. I turn

melodramatically away from the window. The lace drops back into place.

The Contest:
Every morning I'd look from the bed out the window at the Housing Commission flats in the grey rain. Then Mick'd bounce through the door. What a grin! Horrible first thing in the morning. He was one of those short wiry Australians. You could see the sinews in his forearms, the veins in his hands, and when I picture him cuddling with Amy, he looks about four feet tall. He loved to leap onto me in bed. Frustration? Yes, I'd say so. You see, Amy had gone, and we had a competition going to determine who could lead the happiest, most productive life.

He'd confessed this to me: "After a break-up, you're numb for about a week, you feel like a piece of cheese, then the grindstone hits you."

I could see the grindstone wearing him away as he sat in front of me. But he wasn't going to sink. And neither was I. We both loved Amy, along with piles of other blokes including her second husband Rob. She'd taken her long tall American body back to his place. That's when Micko and I began the contest.

It gave him a good psychological advantage to be first up, grinning and writhing on top of me while I was still trying to wake up. I fought back by taking a regular job and, against his one-day-a-week business, it looked pretty productive. As a counter move, Micko began meditating and reading yoga books. He'd be waiting when I returned from work, in the lotus posture on my double bed with as much of a peaceful grin as he could muster onto his ocker-bikie face.

Amy had been gone for a month before we gave up the battle. We commiserated with each other, went to some sad no-women parties and sat around wondering if she'd return.

At night, I'd lie on my double bed stoking the fire and thinking back a few months to the summer when she'd come home with grapes and strange presents, tiny moustache combs, things like that. She was a tall woman but she surrounded herself with anything minute; small fish, little buttons, ornaments.

During the heat wave, she'd get about the house with her long brown hair tied up and just a thin Indian shirt, no underwear; long American legs leading up into that fascinating pubic forest.

We'd often be at home together by ourselves while Mick was out testing new spark plugs or rings on his motorbike. She and Mick rented the room opposite mine. It was actually just a large closet. Amy was so tall, and the room so narrow, that she and Mick could only sleep lengthways. In the mornings, they folded the bed up and placed it against one wall. It was a cosy room; the walls were white like quartz, you could see part of the way into them. Hanging everywhere were small dried flower arrangements and the miniature cartoons she drew. Some of the drawings (framed) were only as big as a matchbox or a cigarette pack, but once you stepped into that frame you'd be in a world, an astral world of cats, grooving along, with the Earth way off in the distance. Her cats had an air of contentment, "freewheelin'" she'd have called it. Even when I'd slip my hand into her pocket to play with her fingers, it felt as if our hands were gliding off through some intergalactic void. You wouldn't believe what went on in the dark in those pockets of hers.

The Brick in the Wall:
One afternoon I came home and found a detailed landscape on a brick. I asked her how she could fit a landscape into a brick and she said: "It was already there. All bricks have them. I just touched that one up."

It makes you wonder, doesn't it, about bricks?

On Sin and Jealousy:
As it grew colder, she took to wearing a long velvet skirt. She'd sit in the kitchen by the wood stove looking like an early pioneer's wife. It was more like a movie then. I'd come in from the cold, ruddy-cheeked, wearing a huge coat, like a bear returning from the blizzard. There she'd sit, quiet and serene. See our eyes meet in sweet wordless welcome.

I'd desire her of course, like the mad animal that I was (in the movie version anyway) and I'd think, here I am with a huge room, a double bed, a fire place, everything a woman needs. It's that type of thinking that can bring you out of a movie flirtation into real trouble, into Sin. And, she already had two lovers.

A Paragraph Demonstrating the Ridiculous Generalization that Technology is Merely an Extension of Man's Nature:
When Rob came over to visit, we'd all sit down to tea. Her lovers were obviously jealous of each other but she seemed to adopt a passive role. It was something we had in common. See? I was always thinking of things we had in common.

Rob and Micko would try to outdo each other with witty pointed jokes. I'd be watching Amy to see how she reacted. She just played it cool. It never really came to the stage where I wished they'd kill each other off, so Amy and I could live in peace, but the tension was building up. There was a definite power struggle.

Mick had a 750 Triumph and Rob a Peugeot racing bicycle of the finest quality. Amy loved speed but also the more sophisticated pleasure of a Sunday-afternoon bike ride. I can imagine her drawing two cats, Mick and Rob. Wiry Mick, hair standing on end, benzining around through stars and Rob, gliding along, carefree, occasionally noticing birds or clouds he passed. And what sort of a cat was I?

The Crunch:

Toward the middle of winter, I'd come home to find Amy reading in my room. She'd have the fire going and there she'd sit in granny glasses and long pioneer skirt. It was like having a wife to come home to. I'd notice the white elegance of her neck. She'd talk about her troubles. The plan was that she might try living with Rob again.

"But how can I leave Micko?" and she'd cry.

God, you don't know what it did to me. I really felt for her, but pity is prone to lust. I kissed her lips sometimes, held her head, and of course, that gave me other ideas.

One Saturday afternoon just before she left, we went walking in the park. Carlton parks are like Sherwood Forest—all these grand English trunks about. Anyway, I was holding her hand and trying to talk her into sleeping with me. She argued against it, but she knew I wasn't all that serious. Still it was good to talk. One of the funny parts of our conversation went like this:

Me: "But, but isn't there a hole somewhere in your argument?"

Amy: "And isn't there a phallus somewhere in yours?"

When we arrived home, she asked me into her narrow room. By this time our discussion was over and we were back to being good friends but I was hoping she'd changed her mind.

I looked at the white skin of her neck and remembered seeing her leaning against the window in her Indian shirt with the sun shining through her pubic hair. She closed the door. I went cold with fear and anticipation, felt the hair rising on the back of my neck. The white of that room.

"What's the matter?" she asked.

"Nothing!"

"I want you to look at this drawing, it's how I feel at the moment."

"Oh, all right."

As usual, it was small—matchbox size. There were cute little hills and a white blob. "What's that?" I asked, pointing to the white part, that looked like a huge amoeba. The title she told me was: *The Great White Forest Going for a Walk.*

"Awww."

Then, quite unexpectedly, it rolled out over me, almost engulfed me, the power of a white forest concentrated into that tiny drawing. You don't expect to find a whole forest in a matchbox. She had caught it just as it came to the crest of a hill and it was leaning a little, like a traveller looking for a place to rest during the night.

I didn't kiss her then, didn't even hug her goodbye; soon after she was gone, and Micko and I began our silly contest.

Phil and Fiona and
John and Judy

When Phil and Fiona moved into the room next door, John and Judy didn't concern themselves too much; "they're hip, they're cool", said John and they maintained their Machine Sex at full throttle.

What is Machine Sex asks the inquiring reader? That's not in the *Kama Sutra*. Let's plug into the conversation of John and Judy, inventors of this fantastic, mechanistic, futuristic pattern of intercourse.

"John, how would you describe the type of sex we have?" asks Judy.

"Well Jude, I've thought a lot about this, it's no good just saying ours is the type of sex that rocks the house, rattles the room and ruins the bed. Considered from the socio-technological angle . . . "

"Yeah, yeah, right!"

" . . . from the viewpoint of total cultural consciousness (and that's the viewpoint from which our sex springs) I'd say we have a kind of Machine Sex."

"Machine Sex?"

"Yeah, that's right Jude."

"Well what is it?"

"I don't exactly know."

"Do you lerv me, Johnny?"

Reader, if you could just imagine, at this moment, a deafening lead guitar break bursting into the room, as Johnny flips back the sheet, leaps up onto the mattress, gyrates like a naked Elvis and begins singing this song for Judy:

"She's a cute little dolly
She sparks like a machine
She fires like a piston
And burns like methyl benzine
So if ya never get ya spanner in
I'd recommend her scene
She's ma rockin rollin steam can baby
She's a can can baby
She cain't say no!
She's ma baby."

The music fades out with a hiss of steam as Johnny collapses on the bed into the socio-technological embrace of Judy.

"Gee they play loud music in there," says Fiona to her beloved Phil, snuggling up to him.

"Yeah and that's not all they do loud."

"Why, what do you mean Phil?"

What Phil is talking about is Machine Sex! Last night while John and Judy were deep into the rhythms of cog, wheel, and piston, Fiona was deep in swinish sleep. Swinish? Why swinish? Swinish because here was Phil, the half-man, half-animal, ready for the greatest orgasm of his life, and beside him lay Fiona, faintly snoring, lying there like a lump of . . . yeah, well. So all he could do was lie on his back smoking, looking up at the ceiling, wondering what it'd be like to be part of a Sex Machine—the Huffings, the Puffings, the I-Knew-I-Coulds.

But he wasn't just an animal, he really loved Fiona. He watched the beautiful child-like face of his WIFE. His wife? Yes! Beg for mercy, you de facto freaks, you cool and trendy readers, Phil and Fiona were one, were spliced, Phil and Fiona were bound in that life-long bond known all over the world as matrimony. So John of the Sex Machine was mistaken about their being "hip and cool". In fact, they were wandering waifs in a world of trendy Johns and Judys, wandering waifs with a huge shameful secret: their marriage.

"Phil, what do you mean, that's not all they do loud?"

"Well, arr . . . O nothing, Fiona."

Note, too, Phil's timidity when it comes to talking about IT.

At the breakfast table:

John: "Sleep well you two?"

"Yes thanks," in chorus.

Fiona: "Gee whizz, you play loud music in there, I'm not complaining or anything, but I didn't think you had a stereo."

John: "We haven't baby. That's Movie Music, it just starts up itself at the right time. You know,

like in the movies. Jude and I make it together don't
we baby."

Judy: "Sure do, honey lamb chop."

John: "And by the way you two, if you hear any
other noises in there, don't worry about it. Ha! Ha!
We're havin' Machine Sex, eh Jude?"

"John don't," smirks Judy.

"No, no, they'll wanna know what's goin' on",
turning to Phil and Fiona, "It's just Machine Sex."

"John please!"

"No Jude, they're cool, they're hip. Aren't ya's."

"Yeah, yeah, we're hip."

And all the time deep down inside their bodies
the fingers of worry are fidgeting with their emotional warts as they ask themselves why they can't
be hip.

Back in their room they hold this conversation:
"We're not hip are we Phil?"

"No."

"Do you want to be hip, Phil?"

Phil doesn't answer, he's engrossed in his *Book
of Exotic Diseases.* Phil has an avid interest in
parasites and pathology. And he still has his stamp,
butterfly, and coin collection. But at the moment,
he's reading about a woman who died after aphids
made their way up her nose and nested in her brain.
Rose sniffing had been her occupation. Apparently
the aphids came from the roses. Beside the story was
a photograph.

"Look at this Fiona."

"Ooooo what is it?"

"A picture of a woman's brain with aphids in it.

After she died there was a post-mortem which found her brain like that."

"Gee whizz. How did they get into her brain?"

"She was a rose sniffer."

"Oh . . . Phil? What's Machine Sex?"

"It's what John and Judy have I suppose."

"Is that what you heard last night, you poor dear?"

"Yes. It must have been. It sounded like a machine, very noisy."

"And what were you thinking about?"

"Nothing."

"Come on, what were you thinking?"

"I was thinking they must be really enjoying themselves to make so much noise."

"Would you like to do it with her?"

"I didn't think that."

"Do you still love me Phil, even though we don't have Machine Sex?"

"Yes Fiona. I do."

Reader, if you'd like to imagine some kind of violin concerto, please do. Make some music for these two wandering waifs, bound by marriage but still truly in love.

Next door: "Nice music! Violins and cellos. What is it? Bach? Mozart? Do you know Johnny?"

"Nupe. Give me rock-n-roll anyday,

   Give it to me anyway

   Hey! Hey! Hey! Baybay!"

And leaving his drawing board, he prances over to Judy who's lying seductively on the couch reading *How to Improve Your Dreams with a Macro Diet.*

He grabs her by the wrist, wiggles his hips as a wailing lead break penetrates into the room.

> When I get inside her motor, I know I'm gonna hit the ton,
> Whack the key in the ignition, she goes orf like a gun,
> I wave goodbye to my mama, I'm driving a big cream bun.
> She's ma rockin rollin steam can baby.
> She's ma can can baby, she cain't say No!
> She's ma baby.

Again, there's a hiss of steam as he collapses onto the couch and he and Judy begin their wild mechanical intercourse.

Next door:

"What's that noise Phil?"

"That's it Fiona. That's Machine Sex."

"Oh!"

Now reader, if you dare, follow me into the room where the thumping and pounding and rasping of the Sex Machine is in full swing, follow me, not as a pervert, but to take a quick sneak look at Johnny's drawing board. What's there? Calculations, reader. I don't expect you'll figure them out. I know what they're all about: I know everything that happens here. This mathematical exercise was aimed at determining the number of times John and Judy have done IT. And that number is three hundred and eighty-one, plus or minus five.

The pounding and puffing stops, the machine bodies of John and Judy exude hisses of steam and smoke. Just before we go, I'll make a correction on the drawing board: three hundred and eighty-two, plus or minus five.

Next door:

"What are you thinking Phil?"

"Nothing."

"Really? Are you sure you're not wishing we could have Machine Sex?"

"You know, I suppose it'd be good if we could. But I wasn't really thinking that. I was wondering how many times we'd done it."

"Oh!"

Now who was it who said you couldn't have sex with the same person more than four hundred times and still enjoy it? Masters and Johnson? Comfort? Reich? Does it matter? Is it true?

Phil, unfortunately, has heard the rumour and he's inclined to believe it. He believes Machine Sex is impossible with Fiona. This depresses him from time to time. He thinks about Other Women. This frightens him, so he delves again into pathology, the fate of rose sniffers, and anything else to keep his mind off the all-important topic. But it remains, an itchy pimple in the brain. He surveys the years of married life ahead, how wasted they appear. How sexless and bare. A pale uneventful future. All the magazine covers mention The Ultimate Orgasm. Will he ever have one?

Two weeks later: two weeks, working on an average of 1.5 a day, this means Johnny and Judy are close to the four hundred mark. John is tense—a hormone imbalance due to faulty sex during the night. Does he need a new woman? He's even thought he could be homosexual.

At the breakfast table:

John: "Sleep well you two?"

In chorus: "Yes thanks."

John: "You're very quiet sleepers. Since you've been here, we've heard nothing from your room but violin music. Not even a full-blooded snore."

Phil, angering: "What do you mean?"

John: "Well, you know . . . "

Phil: "No, I'm afraid I don't know."

John: "Don't you two ever . . . "

Phil: "Ever what?"

John: "You know . . . d'ya want us to come in and show ya how it's done?"

Jude: "John please! It's none of our business."

John: "By Christ it is our business. It's them, it's them who've fucked up our Machine Sex."

Fiona: "Oh!"

"Oh ya fucken self!" says John.

The next day a large heavy packing case arrives at the door. It's for Phil.

"What is it?" asks John.

"It's a heater, one of the new models," says Phil.

"But it's summertime!"

"Well you've got to be ready."

"Yeah, I suppose. I'll give you a hand. Christ, it's heavy."

They drag it into Phil's room. Phil says "thanks", Fiona says "oh", John gives her a dirty look.

It's getting on towards midnight now, the couples have retired to their separate bedrooms. Phil's squeezing his pimples at the mirror. His parasite books are stacked neatly away. The light goes out in John and Judy's room and there's a settling creak from their bed.

Indeed it has become a quiet house since the demise of John and Judy's passion. They made it to four hundred and two, but now only an occasional muffled conversation from their room. No rock-n-roll.

As Phil steps over to switch out the light, we notice a leer of excitement in his eye, a sparkle.

In the kitchen, the quiet ticking of the clock, the scuffle of mice—intimate and cosy night noises. We pass through the house now with the silent, ever-watchful eye of the author, like a camera's eye. Not even the mice know we're here, they nibble the crumbs on the table, move round the honey jar. I love this type of thing. The moonlight coming through the window, the curtains blowing slightly in the breeze, all the lights out—suburbia in slumber. But let's not get carried away, let's keep this thing moving, let's hear a furtive tinkering.

It comes from Phil and Fiona's room and as we move through their door, like a spirit, we see them naked and whispering in the moonlight, stepping lightly round a strange contraption. Fiona looks radiant tonight. But, this kinky stuff is no scene for us. As we turn to leave, we notice on the floor in a small pile pieces of torn package. With our omniscience we can—just—piece together the label:

> *Th   ew   electric ignit   ass fibre*
> *o u b l e   u l a t e d   e x   M a c h i n e : V e n u s*
> *Trap.   neve   urn   back   aft   passi   th*
> *400   ark!*

How discreet.

TALES OF HORROR AND RESURRECTION

The Legend of Barp Doo-Arp

The Legend of Barp Doo-Arp and his ever-faithful pillion Studsy, comes to us out of the Bodgie Era.

The one thing Barp and Studsy always wanted to do was make it to Heaven. To do that, they would have done anything. There was only one condition, they wanted to do it on Barp's Harley Davidson. They'd have foregone molls and malteds, they'd have given the arse to rock-n-roll, and their studs to the Salvation Army. Just that one thing they wanted from the Lord, to make it up there on Barp's Harley.

Barp could still remember the first time he whacked his leg over the saddle of that machine. Barely out of puberty and here he was taming a great hot throbbing beast between his legs; laying her into the corners. Hit the ton first night out.

It wasn't long after the initiation that Barp Doo-Arp had a vision. He remembered it still, in detail; it stood out in his dark past like the lights of the local milk bar.

*I was heading down this strip a tar; flying along,
and before I realized, the dial was nudging a
hundred. But the Harley was still only purring.
Next thing, I was off the road, ridin smooth as hell.
Then I hears this rock-n-roll coming at me from way
up in the distance. Couldn't see a thing, just hear
Elvis croonin his guts out, from somewhere up ahead
in the pitch black. Suddenly I see a juke box, floatin
in space, doin a circle ahead of me. I could see I
was going to have to ride through the circle. Just
before I reach it, Elvis comes fizzing out of the box
like a genie, and there was this glitter flickering all
about him. I can see his eyes now, smiling the way
they do on the cover of* **Blue Hawaii.** *And he says
to me "You can make it boy. Go man go." And there
was this chorus of angels all singing out my name
"Barp Doo-Arp, Barp Doo-Arp". Then Elvis was
singing again:*

> *But Barp stay away
> From a Holden F.J.
> Don't make a lay
> In a Holden F.J.*

*I was back on the road again, still thinking this info
over in my brain. I pulled in at the Hot Box to have
a malted and chat with Valerie. She was the first
I told about it.*

Valerie's style was basically a self-conscious Patty
Duke. She worked nights at the Hot Box saving up
to buy a car and she spent a lot of money on fish-

n-chips. Every time she ate fish-n-chips she'd think of Patty Duke. Patty Duke would never eat fish-n-chips. Suffering thus, she'd tear a hole in the warm newspaper and finger around for them. She dreamed of the day her acne would be gone, a white veil soft over her face and through the tears of happiness she would see Barp, standing proud at the altar rails. Yes ladies and gentlemen, TRUE LOVE.

Valerie was thrilled to hear of Barp's heavenly ambitions. She told him to go see Tungsten at The Foundry. He was the bikies' spiritual father.

On the way Barp thought over his chances for a lay with Valerie. "She's plain but I reckon she thinks I'm all right."

At The Foundry, the atmosphere was quiet and peaceful, the scent of 20/30 incense thick in the air. Barp moved in under the high galvanized iron roof. Along the pews, the Harleys and Hondas sat regally, their chromed carbies silently displaying the high piety of their rank. Up on the altar under the powerful flood lights Tungsten performed the opening rituals of Maintenance. Soon the service began at full throttle. Barp reverently took a pew on the sleek "Blue Heaven", folding his leather gloves in his lap.

With superhuman grace Tungsten laid himself along the saddle of Cherabim and suddenly, as if in ecstasy, eyes upwards to the rafters, he jerked back the accelerator. The roar was tremendous: Tungsten vibrated like a huge lump of jelly but held on. The sound flared round his body, consuming his godly stature. His chrome helmet shone with a white supernatural light. Incense filled The Foundry, and through the gutsy vro-o-oom Barp heard once again the chorus of angels. This time they sang his name, tier upon tier reaching back into the heights of the rafters, they sang in harmonies, in convolutions of gloria. *Barp Doo-Arp, Barp Barp Doo-Arp.*

Then silence, but for the peaceful tinkering of a spanner.

Tungsten freed himself of the helmet and came down the aisle. Only now could Barp see the pock marks on his face, the humanness of Tungsten. Seconds before this was a being whose true home was within the blue flame of a blow torch.

"What ails thee, Barp?"

"I've had a vision Tung, of angels, of Elvis. I want to make it to heaven on the Harley, and Studsy wants to come too. Tung, I don't care about anything else. What can I do?"

"Barp, you've been called. You're a special bikie. I'll do all I can to help you. For the moment, take this set of Sidchromes. Service your bike well. Maintenance, Barp, Maintenance and more Maintenance. It's what the world needs most today. Elvis go with you."

Barp took the Sidchromes and moved out from under The Foundry roof.

It came to pass that one evening Barp and Studsy went to the Elite drive-in to see a Buddy Holly movie. Both of them throught it was great, though Studsy had trouble seeing from his pillion seat directly behind Barp's head. He knew he shouldn't, but he began looking round at the hot rods, actually taking pleasure in the chrome, the widies, the venetian blinds in the back windows. Suddenly he saw it, the hot red F.J. It was the chrome lightning strip along the side which sucked him in. Just to touch it! At the driver's seat was a little lady with bee-sting lips and breasts pulled up like a couple of pine cones. Studsy was still trying to look away but when he did and saw only the back of Barp's greasy head, he wilted and turned back, ready to be consumed by the pleasures of immorality.

It was the pine cones now that got him looking back. She was bopping them up and down to the tune of "That'll Be the Day".

When the screen flashed up "Intermission", gold letters on red velvet, Barp looked round to grin at Studsy. But wayward Studsy, with his elbow on the front window of the F.J., was boring that lady to tears. Barp saw that immediately. Studsy was okay if you understood him, but sometimes . . . no class. Barp was going over to apologize.

As the sounds of Studsy's gutteral laughter die out Barp introduces himself.

"Hi, me name's Barp Doo-Arp."

"And what can I do for you, chicken?"

"Shove over, let me show ya how a man can tickle a machine like this."

Seconds later, and the mags on that F.J. are rumpling the carpet of the drive-in theatre. Studsy is left pulling stones out of his complexion as that mean machine rumbles like a red reptile through the gates out onto the highway.

Her name's Candy Sidchrome, and she's still bored to tears. Barp plays it cool. He doesn't speak but begins laying that car into the corners. They take a few on two wheels, slide sideways on four. And she sits there chewing gum, like she's at a lecture on heart disease. Barp spins out a few more times and pulls in at a little parking spot, known by the local boys as the Passion Pit. She doesn't speak. He looks at her pine cones out of the corner of his eye. Suddenly, he grabs her gum-chewing jaw and whacks his hot lips across her mouth. She warms up a bit.

Meanwhile Studsy is back at the Elite. Everyone's gone. The only sound coming across the gravel slope is the tinkering of Barp's Sidchrome. Maintenance.

Is friendship so paltry? Is TRUE LOVE really to be had with Candy? Is she the F.J. lady? Or Heaven? And what about Studsy, alone all night at the Elite, with Black Bishop and the Toebars riding the area? But if Candy *is* Heaven, Studsy can't be pillion, or even sidecar man . . .

Barp was putting these questions to himself in a booth at the Hot Box and trying to soothe his mind with a bit of Elvis—"Wooden Heart". Barp wondered what his was made of.

The next thing Studsy appeared at the booth, his face haggard.

"You bastard Barp. Leaving me all night with the Harley. Scared shitless the Black Bishop might turn up. And what about that cruddy Candy Sidchrome. I thought you knew better than to go off in an F.J."

"Studsy, I'm sorry about last night. Take it out on me, man, but not on Candy. Listen, with a name like Sidchrome she can't be bad. Her dad is the Sidchrome magnate, the Spanner King. She's a free ticket through the Pearly Gates."

"Barp, do you know what you're doing? She drives an F.J. That's enough for me."

"You're jealous and thick. Tungsten himself uses Sidchromes. She's a winner, Studsy, and I'm ridin her through to the finish . . . with or without you."

It was then that Studsy sacrificed his first malted, by throwing it over his spiritual brother. He walked out and caught a bus home.

Barp was really worked up, mainly because he'd seen Elvis in a shot like this. Valerie rushed over to calm him down. But the sounds of "Devil with an Angel Face" encouraged him to finish the scene. He shoved her aside, kidded himself the strawberry malted was blood, and went for the bike. Valerie, pulling her bruised hip off the edge of the juke box, rushed outside, tears in her eyes, dishcloth in hand. She wiped up a little puddle of strawberry malted which somehow represented the last she'd ever see of Barp, and went inside, thinking of the only comfort she had—a warm bag of chips.

Once on the road, the malted on Barp's person began to flow backwards in little pink trickles.

Valerie was still massaging her chip-inflated thigh. But Barp was thinking of another doll, a hep cat doll—Candy Sidchrome. Twisting the accelerator like a mad dog, he leapt along the highway, his head cuddling low to the petrol tank.

"R-r-r-r I'd like to give her a valve grind."

Sooner or later this type of thinking brought him round to Candy's place. He stunk of pink blood, but a man like Barp doesn't give a damn. The Harley roared just one more time before Big Daddy Barp lifted his leg off her. The sounds of "Kansas City" throbbed through the house. He took everything real slow. A man like Barp doesn't go to the front door. He stood tall in the street, taking a long time with his gloves, acting like he didn't even know the house was there. The music stopped. Candy came to the front door and opened up.

"Come on in, Barp. Meet Daddy."

Meanwhile Studsy is sitting at home picking studs out of his leather jacket and blackheads out of his nose. His nose is big and red.

That night Barp and Candy are cuddling up in the front seat of the F.J., watching Elvis croon his way through *Acapulco*. It's on at the Elite, and there's this part where Elvis is wobbling up to this little doll with a low-cut dress. Barp is pretty excited and greases his hair back, just like Elvis does. Elvis is smiling through the front window of every little machine down there before him. Barp slips his strong arm, the one with the "Death before Dishonour" tattoo, round Candy's waist. He can feel some kind of underwear tight across her body. She sniggers and snuggles into him like the pink little gum-chewing baby she is. Elvis becomes less important. Out of the two hundred and fifty cars down there before him now, he is idol for only twenty. Candy's red F.J. is one of the two hundred and thirty others. His blue-light smile reaches out across the drive-in onto an endless array of empty front seats. He breaks into song and the angels sing *Barp Doo-Arp, Barp Barp Doo-Arp.* But Barp's body is stinking of sweat and petrol—and Candy loves it. His hand moves up her leg to the broad expanse of her thigh. She giggles, takes the opportunity for a last gobble at the gum, moves it to the corner of her mouth and sticks it there. Barp's Sidchrome is trying to break out of the tool box. Then he feels it, just past her thighs, the cold metal. He lifts up her skirt and there, shining in the dark—a pair of chrome-plated panties. The car is rocking with the laughter of that devil with an angel face. And Elvis is still smiling.

Meanwhile Studsy is paying a visit to Tungsten's Foundry. He finds him as usual down on his knees, maintaining the bikes. He pleads with Tungsten to help save the wayward Barp. Tungsten has never before ridden into the territory of the Black Bishop —not since the days of the Harley Crusades anyway. But Barp is a special bikie, and Tungsten, risking full scale gang warfare, dons chrome helmet and silver gloves. This mission requires the services of Blue Heaven, the flashest bike in the fleet. His big heavy boot moves to the kick start, and before long he and Studsy have left behind a puff of the pungent blue incense.

The Elite is just ahead. So far so good, no sign of the Black Bishop. Blue Heaven purrs through the gates. They spot the red F.J. quickly; Studsy dismounts and runs over. Candy is sitting alone in the front, chewing gum. She winds the window up when she sees Studsy coming. No sign of Barp.

"Where is he, Candy?" he murmurs.

"Where is he, Candy?" he says.

"Where is he?" he yells.

Then there is the familiar roar of Black Bishop's gang, the dazzling headlights.

"Hey Chrome Dome," shouts Black Bishop.

During the ensuing battle, the sounds of "Don't Step on My Blue Suede Shoes" peel off the silver screen and fall like soft autumn leaves down through the slashing and screaming.

Tungsten and Studsy never made it back. And after that, Candy Sidchrome hung up her cold metal panties and put an end to her hep cat game. Barp had fled in horror. He located his Harley, but didn't have the spunk for a good rap. He just coasted on down to the Hot Box. Valerie was still there, mixing malteds.

"Hi Barp! Gee, Whassa matter?"

"Baby, I need ya."

This is just what Valerie has been dreaming of for so long. Barp coming in and saying "I need ya".

"Just hang on a sec, Barp, I'll clean up and take

you home." *Bwerp Bwerp* . . . "Hello Hot Box,
Valerie Crimple here."

"Dis is de Black Bishop. We's cremating a coupla
Barp's cronies over at the Elite after the show.
Thought we'd ring up and invite him over. See ya,
Val baby."

This news struck Barp below the belt. He
collapsed off the stool, went close to splitting his
head open on the juke box. And across the dark
blanket of his mind he beheld a vision of Tungsten
and Studsy (red nose looking real proud now) riding
that beautiful machine, Blue Heaven. Their
pathway led ever upwards through grand lumps of
cumulus and nimbus. Once, they stopped to look
back at him, kindly, and as they roared away the
Sidchromes spilled from the saddle-bags, began
falling end on end slowly back to Barp. And
Tungsten's chrome helmet disappeared through the
heavenly landscape.

Barp woke with his head resting on Valerie's lap;
she had some hot chocolate for him. He spoke to
her of the vision, the slow-descending Sidchromes,
and she comforted him by reading from Tungsten's
Manual: "A bikie is always ready to die . . ."

Feeling better now, Barp stood up tall in his long
black corduroys.

"Come on, I'll take you home."

"What sort a machine you got, Val?"

"A Holden F.J."

The Hound
of Heaven

From celestial clouds the clergy bombard me with
dog carcass and black-red roses. To save my soul
from the devil.

I love the devil who walks with me like a shadow
underneath concrete paths, follows me like a shark
swimming underground. We often have a laugh
together. The world's such a funny place. He knows.

The clergy's sad pudgy faces peer over the cloud
rims eager to perceive the results of their meat and
flower evangelism. The roses fall apart and deep
down at their petal bases are myriads of Finger
Things—ugly little creatures like amputated fingers,
growing on each other. They wiggle and shout like
dwarfs. Devil fella love them!

Dog carcass is very intricate theology indeed,
snout, claws, paws, canines, doggy sinews, throat,
vertebrae, dog breath—beautifully put together. It
splatters on the concrete which is the division
between my world and you-know-who-else's.

A Fair-Dinkum
Yarn

Once upon a time, there were two men who were
Real Australians. They lived in the ruddy heat of
Real Australia, where all True Bushmen are found.
They were tall, strong sun-tanned men whose blue
piercing eyes could penetrate for miles across the
hazy plains into the Blue and Distant Mountains.

Their names were Jim Price and Jim Price. They
both had the same name. (In Real Australia if
something works once, True Bushmen will do it
again and again and again. They hardly ever make
mistakes.) One of the Jims, whose face was like an
old boot, had fought for and saved Real Australia
from the fiendish invasion of the Nips. He then
returned to Real Australia and accidentally "fucked
his way to fatherhood". The other Jim was born
into a "free and bloody bonza-beautiful country"—
Real Australia, and Jim was proud of it. Jim was
also "real proud" of Jim and in turn the other Jim
thought the old man "the best bastard for miles".
(There were no other bastards for miles.)

But aharr, only thirty years after the blind and

buck-toothed Nip had been driven from the shores, and Jim and Jim were under the dastardly spell of Demon Drink. Doesn't a man deserve any peace! Jim and Jim, once capable and clear-eyed, were now changed into the toadish form of pregnant men. Their bellies swelled hopelessly beyond their control.

"It could happen to anyone," they said comforting each other.

But that wasn't the end of their woes. A kind of morning sickness caught up with them nearly every night. They accepted it with the serenity and good cheer of child-bearing women who realize that eventually it's all worth it. Were it not for this high-minded attitude, they may never have won the respect of the Fairy Godmother. She watched them lovingly, night after night as they writhed in spasms, hurling over the railings of the Grand Emporium Parthenon Pub, known to the locals all over Real Australia as simply "The Grand". This wasn't for the likes of the Fairy Godmother, she supped at "The Queens", nudge, nudge.

Inside that jolly tavern The Grand, Jim and Jim caroused with merriment, spilling the froth with carefree Joy and Gay Abandon, the open-legged barmaids.

"What big hands you have Jim!"

"Yep! All the better for drinking with my dear," he'd say obscuring a midi in his huge and brawny fist.

"What powerful winks you got Jim," would intimate Gay Abandon timidly.

"All the better to fuck you with my dear," would be the irresistible retort.

"And what a big mouth!"

"All the better fer sinking piss . . . hey wait on Gay, you havin a go at me. Watch it, love."

(It's hard for a man to be agreeable when he's pregnant but even harder for a wolf to dress up like a grandmama, don't you reckon?)

The Jims were marvellous at conversation. They'd always know what to say. And they'd never forget conversations.

"Like I mean Jim, if a conversation works you use it again don't ya? Otherwise y' end up saying things people don't expect. Catches em off guard, [more intimately] and you can really hurt a man like that."

"Yeah, you're right mate. Thanks fer pointing that out. It's good being able to talk serious to someone eh? We can talk deep," said Jim moving closer.

"Yeah, well not too close mate, and no deeper than a ten ounce glass a piss," said Jim pushing Jim to a safc distance. "Don't reckon I want to be known as a poofter. Next, they'll be tellin us to do our drinking over at The Queens. Anyway, time fer a bark isn't it?"

"Right O!" said Jim, gruffly, trying to sound like a man. They stumbled outside.

Jim and Jim had an ideal barking set-up. They loved to do it. One Jim'd grip the rails, leaning over as far as he dared.

"Come on mate, further, arse up now."

The other Jim'd climb on top and reach round to shove his finger down his mate's throat, at the same time bouncing up and down to help move it from the tum.

"Harder mate harder! Bounce harder! Push yer fucken finger right down."

Then it'd all come at once in some superhuman hurl, a spasm of ecstacy.

"BARRRK!!!"

Sighs of pleasure and relief.

"Awwww . . . gi-normous, mate. Works every time."

"Gotta be quick, get your finger out."

"Righto your shot."

(Children, see how brave are the Jims in the face of this Demon? Take courage from their bravado and comradeship. Truly, that's all it is.)

Each night the Fairy Godmother, disguised as a wandering shearer with bluey, would watch the Jims as they helped each other through the tribulations imposed by Drink's wicked spell.

> From Brewery the beer makes you piss and
>   fart
> Winds a tube around yer heart,
> Let cocks go limp, piss in this glass
> Now drink it again, it's your mate's, first
>   class!

Drink had often pulled Fairy Godmother into the demon world, where mangy blue heelers nipped her ankles, where ockers stubbed out cigarettes in her face, where the whole bar guffawed and booted her outside shouting POOFTER. She knew well the powers of piss.

126

Many times she had tussled with Drink and lost, had sunk into the alcoholic darkness at the back of the shearing shed (vomiting down behind the bed) eventually waking up stinking, lying in her own pale vomit. But those were the days when she feared her own Fairy Godmother powers. She couldn't understand the magic in her wand. Only now was she coming to realize the powers she could command over Drink. Her wand was accumulating a massive force, like ten tonnes of whipped cream.

If anyone could help the Jims, she believed it was herself. She knew Drink's disguise: The Breast with the Cracked and Bleeding Nipple. And watching the Jims' ritual over the rail she realized "all they needed was a good bang" (as they call it in Real Australia). "Just a little poof" she thought to herself.

But little did Fairy Godmother know that she was just a pawn in Drink's masterplan. He had her by the balls, or by the magic wand as they say in spritely circles.

The next evening Jim and Jim, still labouring under a strange power, found themselves barging through the doors of The Grand Emporium Parthenon Pub. They called for schooners, winked erotically at Gay Abandon, and began feeding the alcoholic-demon embryos curled in their respective bellies. They also began a conversation whose words they hadn't forgotten.

"Remember that old FC, Jim?"

"Yeah."

"Drove that for a week without a drop a oil in it you know. Just wouldn't die. Even when I was good to it, I only fed her with used oil. Fucken good motors them."

(One of the pasttimes of True Bushmen is putting motors to the ultimate test.)

Meanwhile in her room over at The Queens, Fairy Godmother changed herself from a bleary-eyed weather-worn swaggy into a beautiful buxom Fairy Godmother. Six long petticoats of fine lace with a wonderful rustle to it, a long red and black gown (low-cut), three pounds of dark black hair piled on top of her head, purple eye-shadow with a tasteful splash of glitter, and of course, underneath it all, the magic wand, holding a power of whipped cream. Making a final adjustment at her bust, she swaggered out into the street.

Jim and Jim had just stumbled outside for their nightly bark. Good timing Fairy Godmother!

"Hey Jim, look at that."

"Yeah, the boobs . . . wonder how she keeps her back straight."

"She's comin over ere. Let's piss off."

"Wait on mate. Never let a woman scare ya. No matter how big her boobs are."

Fairy Godmother: "Wonderful night boys."

Jim: "Yeah, good night fer a . . . fer a drive."

Fairy Godmother: "A drive where?"

Jim: "In to the bush . . . ah I mean out along the highway, up into the hills. Beautiful up there on a night like this. We can go in me new ute. Jim buy us half a dozen will ya? I'll escort the lady to the car."

Fairy Godmother: "Thank you."

They headed out across the warm, still plains into the Blue and Distant Mountains, now dark under the twinkling stars of the Southern Cross, the Milky Way and others. Demon Drink was with them, winking in the froth and bubbles of the half dozen on the seat, waiting to be released.

"Jimmy, knock the top off one a them will ya? Where's ya manners? Give the lady a drink."

Jimmy removed the top with his teeth and Drink came forth with a hiss of white spew. Pushing the bottle between his lips, the demon beer foamed into his mouth, he guzzled faster till he felt it rush into his stomach. Then sitting back, he thought how nice it was going to be peeling off each petticoat slowly, then the panties. He was having first dip this time. Jim always went first; not this one, I mean a fair fuck's a fair fuck.

The ute left a trail of dust as it sped along, eventually climbing the mountains, entering between the boulders like a quick and angry goanna. They stopped the car. Jim threw a bottle into the dark and listened for the smash. It landed and bounced, without breaking.

"Fuck it," he muttered to himself.

Fairy Godmother: "Excuse me boys, I'm off for a wee."

Jim: "Right."

They listen to her tiny shoes crunching away through the stones and twigs.

"Listen mate, I'm first in this time."

"Fuck that!"

The heat of the demon rushing within them.

"Tell ya what, we'll skoll a bottle each, the man who finishes first, goes in first."

"Righto. No spillage."

Jim won.

"Seeya later, she's been away long enough. Which way'd she go?"

The winner lurched off into the dark, chucking his bottle aside. Meanwhile Demon assumed the guise of The Breast with the Cracked and Bleeding Nipple, and appeared to Jim. He ran toward it like a child, weeping and gurgling, held it and began sucking, receiving blood and beer. He sucked till he vomited and pissed in his pants. He passed out, woke and sucked again, occasionally weeping. No one came to change his nappy.

Jim was under the spell of the Fairy Godmother. He pushed his hands into the neck of her dress and pulled out her breasts. Pushing her over, he lay on her, forcing her breasts around his head. She pulled up her gown and began moving rhythmically against his body, quicker and more urgent till finally she reached climax. Jim couldn't get it up.

He put his hand to her crutch and felt there the magic wand, surrounded by whipped cream. He couldn't stand it, anything but getting it on with a poofter. He hallucinated. He saw a wolf's head with a granny cap peering out between a vagina's lips. "All the better . . . " Pulling up his pants as he scrambled off, he swore and cursed and soon returned with sharp rocks (one in each hand). He used them to break the Fairy Godmother's head.

When he returned, he found Jim lying in the dirt,

surrounded by spew and broken beer bottles. They argued about who should drink the last bottle.

"Give it here Jimmy or I'll have yer balls for cufflinks."

Jim broke it over Jim's head.

Episode Six in the Saga
of the Almighty:
Hippo Eats Drowned Horse

People tell me God is dead. And I almost kill myself laughing at them. Don't they know? Aren't they up with his latest, greatest manifestation?

They say He's a Drowned Horse and point to Him through the Celestial Dishwater, bloated and rolling around on the bottom. I can see the Drowned Horse, but can't they see what's eating it? The water is a little murky and grey but when you're desperate to be suckled at His breast, you look a little harder.

In my spiritual quest, I sucked on an open intestine which had come toward me like a snake, dull and white. And being ingested through that mass of whirling bowel, I came into the Grey Waters. Strange, fatherly noises surrounded my head which I had voluntarily dismembered. Thus I entered into the realms of God. This was a surprise, you don't expect to find God, but you see, I'd forgotten His reputation for Relentless Omnipotence.

There He was, that fun-loving God, in His large grey Hippo pose, gnawing flesh off the Drowned Horse.

Christ and Crutches

The bastard had me cornered for a while. I mean how silly can you get to be cornered by a Jesus freak, by one of The Chosen. Honestly, I was ashamed of myself.

How could I let it happen?

He must have heard me and Terry the night before talking through the wall to each other. We often do that. A mark of friendship, of love. Being your usual maladjusted Australian male, we can't just say "goodnight mate it's been a lovely day, pleasant dreams". No, it has to be more casual, more laid back. Hugging him goodnight would be fine by me but it has to be kept latent doesn't it: the homosexuality.

Anyway instead of that, we just usually abuse each other. I call him a cockhead, a king turd or something like that and he returns the compliments with similar warmth. Then, off to sleep.

Isaac (he renamed himself after a religious experience) listened to us one night, he must have. It was the night we were talking about wet dreams.

"Pleasant dreams," I said through the wall, trying to be friendly.

"Wet dreams," Terry said, trying to be crass.

"Yeah!" I was alert immediately, "I've never had one mate."

"I had three in one night. On the train up from Sydney."

"What was it like?"

"Terrible."

"Yeah! Do you have orgasms and everything?"

"Hey?" The wall is pretty thick.

"Do you have orgasms and everything!" I shouted.

"You've really never had one?"

"No."

See, I just thought you woke up in the morning and found out then. I didn't realize there was any mileage in it, didn't realize it could be fun. I'm slightly disappointed with myself. Here I am a quarter of a century on this Earth and as yet haven't experienced that ever so common phenomenon, the wet dream.

"Is it fun? How can I have one?"

"Just go to sleep mate. Try it."

I turned over and shut my eyes hoping for visions of erotic splendour. Nothing.

The next night, the crunch came. He set the trap. It was just before I was heading off to bed. I didn't want to be sitting there with him at that hour, alone.

Eleven o'clock. I know how Christians work. At eleven they start talking, a few cups of coffee, midnight comes around and the world is a horrible hole of suffering and sin. (It's got nothing to do with the fact that you're dog-tired and high on caffeine.) I bet there've been thousands of people converted between midnight and 1 a.m. who wake up the next morning wondering where it's all gone. Just like being raced off at a party. They seduce you into getting down on your knees, they plaster their hands all over your head, you start weeping and praying, they call for the intercession of Christ . . .

I was onto it. But Isaac was cunning.

"Denis," he said, with a far-reaching piercing look in his eye. And I hated the way he said my name.

"Denis," he said and looked at me as if my heart would break apart and bleed and beg for a prayer to save my suffering.

"Denis," he said, "do you ever pray before you go to sleep?"

"Nuh." Maybe I do, maybe I don't. But whose fucken business is that?

"Denis, do you ever have wet dreams?"

"Look Isaac, I'm quite happy with the calibre of my dreams thank you. My subconscious is as lively as anybody's."

You see, he'd hit me in a soft spot. I'm a quiet man but I react.

"But Denis, do you have wet dreams?"

"Nuh."

At this, his eyes brightened; shone. I didn't

understand why. Surely there's no morality con-
nected with wet dreaming. Surely he didn't admire
me because, even while dreaming, I could maintain
a lofty outlook. Even the Christian Brothers aren't
that radical. They used to say to us (as we sat there
with little shaved bullet heads and guilty, embarrassed faces): "Boys, your natural urges will take
care of themselves in sleep." I didn't know what they
were talking about; but obviously they were giving
deference to that wild animal, the subconscious.
"You may have wet dreams but it's not your fault,
boys," they could have said, "we are not perfect
creatures."

Isaac was on a different tack.

"That's great. That's great!" He almost shouted.
Then he had second thoughts. He lowered his head
closer to the kitchen table as if to sneak under my
line of vision. "Do you ah . . . masturbate?" he
asked, like only a Christian could.

"Yep. Course I do." It took years but I finally
achieved an almost celebratory attitude toward
masturbation. I found peace.

He was shocked. "Oh, I thought you were
diverting your energies into another area."

"No, not me."

This was his big chance. He was eager to save
a soul. "It's an incredible battle."

"What battle?"

"Against the flesh!"

"What flesh," I asked, knowing full well what
particular piece of flesh he referred to.

"The flesh of our bodies, Denis."

The way he said FLESH. His mouth and tongue slavered with excitement. The meat of his lips worked overtime on that word, contorted.

"There's the Flesh, the soul (which is God), the spirit, the will, and the Flesh."

"That's two fleshes. Jesus mate, I've only been given one."

"Denis, it's an incredible battle."

"No it isn't. Not if you don't fight it."

I looked at the clock. It was getting on. Isaac was following the typical pattern of the evangelists. Get them tired, get them down, hold their heads under the murky waters of their sin, then when they're nearly dead, let them up and show them a crucifix. Christ has saved you.

Friends, fight back. Don't take it. Push the hedonist philosophy and God help you.

"Denis, stop masturbating, allow yourself to experience a wet dream. Masturbating is a crippling thing [that's a new one], a wet dream is a growing experience."

Masturbators, listen to that line again will you? Put it up in lights on the billboards of your mind. "The Wet Dream—A Growing Experience."

"Okay," I said, "I'll try it."

"But you have to give up masturbating."

"Yeah. For how long though."

"At least a week or two."

"Jesus."

He cringed at that.

"Well it'd only be a couple of days if you were a real man." (See that! He did have a sense of humour after all.)

"Okay," I said, "I'll give it a week."

I tried to leave the table but he put his hand on me. That's the dangerous time.

"Right mate," I said, "see you in the morning."

"Denis, Christ helps me when temptation comes during sleep. He's always there. I have such strength, but it's only through Him. If some woman tries to seduce my flesh in a dream I call on Him. I can touch His presence and fight off temptation. Oh, I wake during the night, and at times I'm crying out for help. 'Jesus, Jesus, help me.' This morning I woke at four and prayed till dawn. I woke knowing perfectly well that I had to read Corinthians 1.13. Do you know it? It starts 'When I was a child, I spoke like a child . . . ' "

"Yeah, yeah, I know." We had this teacher at school who'd say it all the time. Even now it doesn't make sense. "But you got up at four to read that?"

"Yes. God told me to."

"Jesus no wonder you have to sleep till ten every morning."

"Denis, Jesus is always with me. He is my link to the Father. [He stressed the word "link". Tried to make it sound like a holy word. He ruined it for me. I used to like "link", just the sound of it. But now it's a done-for word.] And around me I have all my Christian brothers, my friends." He spoke as if I had no friends. But anyway, he went on to some powerful symbolism. "Christ is my vertical link with The Father and through Him, I have a horizontal link with my brothers. That makes the

Cross. That's good that is."

Those were his exact words: "That's good that is." What forms a cross is the horizontal-vertical link business. Get it? Fantastic eh? Very very rich.

He was going to continue, but I left him for the joys of my mattress. The last thing he said was "it's an incredible battle, Denis". I was too tired to fight it, too tired to get up to any monkey business. So I went to sleep and my naturally pure subconscious came up with nothing as usual. The bloody thing.

The next morning he was on to me like a ton of hot bricks. At first I thought they were Bibles. I picked one up. A little gold tassel bookmarker dangled out, and on the front was written *The Holy Bible*. But I couldn't open it anywhere, no pages. It was just square and heavy. I came to the conclusion a new type of Christian brick had been made. Ideal for the bedside table, a nice showpiece. They were lying all about me in a dishevelled state, and he was there in his pyjamas like one of those pioneer Christians in a cowboy movie. His jaw was set.

"Denis, it's an incredible battle. How are you?"

All I wanted was to eat my Weet-Bix in peace. I resent people asking me how I am, as if they're expecting me to fall apart. When he asked "how are you?", he didn't mean "good morning, sleep well?", he meant "did you pull yourself last night?"

"Are you asking if I pulled myself last night?"

"Denis!" He came closer. He would have touched me if I'd let him. Get out I'm eating my bloody Weet-Bix.

"No, I didn't mate, I was too tired."

"Good. The Lord's helped you. Rest in Him."

Just then Leo came into the breakfast room. He sensed there were some heavy vibes around. He looked at Isaac and then at me. I'm frank but I'm not so good that I could just say, "Isaac is telling me to stop masturbating so I can have a wet dream." Leo knows I do it, but he doesn't ask for a rundown every morning. See how Isaac had forced that intimacy of his? He had me by the short and curlies. I just looked at Leo; Isaac backed off into his room. He had a look in his eye, "Denis, it's our secret, let's share it together with Christ and grow toward Him." The implication was that Leo was Temptation, part of the old life which I had now shed. What could I do but shrug?

Leo went off into the shower; Isaac put on a tape of angels singing "Gloria". At that hour in the morning you can imagine how angels affect me.

He came in for another probe.

"Did you pray for help?"

"No mate but you'll need to soon."

It was over his head—like most things in his life were. I got up and took my Weet-Bix into the shower with Leo. Anything for some peace. It was fun standing in there, warm, as the steam filled the room.

"It's an incredible battle mate," I said, over the curtain.

"What is?" Leo asked and, receiving no answer, he swished back the curtain and stood there, surrounded by clouds of smoke, in the nick—in the Nick.

A Vegetarian Fantasy

Once upon a time there were two kind-eyed, jolly, middle-aged cattle, Herefords as a matter of fact, Mr. and Mrs. Meadow. They worked quietly and constantly all their lives so now could spend the cold winter nights in their rather comfortable barn.

Mr. Meadow would sit by the fire reading the local evening newspaper, *The Bull Sheet*, while the Mrs. prepared dinner.

"By geez there's some good stock about this season Mildred. Look at that beauty. Well hung don't you think. Have to hire him for a spell, the ladies'll love it."

"Yes Rex darling. He's not a touch on you though," said the flirtatious Mildred.

"Aha, certainly true," retorted the randy Rex.

"Good God! What a terrible thing . . . "

"What Rex? Not another uprising?"

"Yes dear, I'm afraid so."

"Where this time?"

"In the lowland blocks along the east coast."

"The Jerseys again. It's their lack of discipline

Rex, I'm sure of it. They're too kind to the men."

"Oh no!"

"What now?"

"Mildred, men are actually eating the Jerseys. A herd of wild men were discovered three days ago boiling parts of their master's carcass. Bones from three or four other cattle were found scattered about the bush."

"Oh Santa Gertrudis protect us."

"Listen to this: 'A team of psychologists from the Brahman Stud University claim the men are demanding an end to slaughter of their numbers, freedom to roam the land without barbed wire fences, and the liberty to choose their own partners instead of being enclosed with supposedly well-hung playboys. The head psychologist at the University, Mr. Frederick Kikuyu, says the claims have been put to him by an intelligent man believed to be of Australian stock. Apparently the man is highly respected and has been most successful at increasing stock numbers in a very short period. His fertility was highly valued by his last owner, Mr. Alf Couch, a Jersey. The man is now hiding out with a renegade herd in the rugged mountain territory of the Great Divide. Another herd of men which late this morning broke loose from an abattoir in Pimble is believed to be heading towards the Great Divide to join the renegades. The State Pig Department has issued an all-out alert advising the Jerseys to keep a sharp eye on all herds as further break-outs could be expected'."

"Rex, where will it all end?"

"By Christ, they'd better not come out west, I'd shoot every last one a mine rather than let em get loose."

"It's the big ideas those Brahmans have put into their heads Rex, it drives em crazy, sends em scattering all over. Brahman Stud University, they should all be locked up. They're the ones. Don't think we'd ever see any of ours run amok. Take Mary Green for instance, she's a beautiful little girl."

"She was Mildred."

"What do you mean *was*, Rex?"

"You've got a couple of slices off her rump in the frying pan there."

"Oh Rex you didn't."

"Now Mildred, you know we can't afford to be sentimental."

"Oh well Santa Gertrudis! Poor Mary Green. Looks very tender though doesn't it?"

Rex rubbed his tired eyes, settled back in front of the fire and began reading a court report.

"Mr. Justice Fresian today fined Terry Bison of Bison Downs after having found him guilty of buggery. This was Bison's third appearance before the courts. Mr. Fresian told Bison that his behaviour and that of many cattle in today's society gave cause to the renegade herds of men. This was all too common a practice, Mr. Fresian said. The court was also told by Pig Prosecutor Igor Nettle that the female human had been . . . ' "

"Come on Rex, it's ready! . . . You know I heard one of those Brahman's from the Stud say today he believed men were once more highly evolved than cattle."

"Ridiculous," said Rex, popping a juicy morsel into his large head.

SNAPSHOTS

The Shape of Eric Zuckman's Sadness

Geometrical planes are infinite, they intersect and reach out from the Earth like myriads of glass panes.

To take an example, the edge of a skyscraper establishes a plane which moves out infinitely in every direction. This plane in the form of a sheet of glass would cut the Earth in two and continue out into space. The planes reaching out from the surface of a leaf would appear more gentle but more prolific.

Spheres on the other hand are fully enclosed, perfect, self-contained. Eric's plump baby fingers grope with a problem, the sphere, the cone. Somehow the cone reminds him more of Ellen and himself. He knows the sphere is too beautiful, too harmonious. He places it down on the desk, aware that the desk top itself reaches out in every direction like a desert in which he is buried waist deep. His hand reaches for the cone. This is more like the shape of the problem.

"Planes are infinite, we only imagine them divided into segments for the purposes of convenience," said Eric's professor, years back, miles back. Zuckman's professor has a voice which echoes from wall to wall of a prism in Eric's head.

It is always night in Eric's room, he is always just home from the Exchange, he is always just finished thinking about Ellen. He is always lonely.

Note the floorboards in Eric's room, like floorboards drawn into a cartoon, just lines. His overcoat is always rumpled on the floor, like a dog growling. Eric's head is round and fat, includes a balding patch. His eyes and lips are sad, large. When he thinks about geometry he rubs his head with his baby hands. His bottom is plump under the baggy pants.

"A cone, once reaching the apex continues on to form a second cone, a reflection of itself."

Eric's lamp sheds a beam of light over his hunched body, his fingers feeling the surface of the cone before him. The old refrigerator in the corner makes the only noise. Mice with pointed faces live in the dust underneath it. The old fridge is like the back of a fat man's head. Its shadow is black. On Eric's small kitchen table is a squat electric jug with a cracked lid. Note the cracked lid, as if it were drawn in a cartoon. Eric is writing down mathematical formulae. His lips are moving just a little.

Behind him is the porcelain sink. A tap drips into the hole. Zuckman has often tried to glimpse the exact shape of these drops but his eye is not quick enough. Where the soap should be is a squashed cigarette. Loose shreds of tobacco look like worms.

Eric's wrinkled black shoes are under the sink.

"A cone can be cut into no more than four different mathematical shapes."

Eric's clock is broken in half, cracked down the centre, pieces of brass machinery are lying about on the floorboards.

When Ellen came that Sunday they ate toasted cheese sandwiches. The cheese bubbled up under the grill. He made the tea in the squat jug. Ellen tried to see the water boiling through the crack. She put her eye down close.

She looked bright and neat with the scarf across her hair. Later she took it off. He noticed her eyes were clear from the side. She said she liked the walls, how white they were. Her breasts were round under the blouse, her legs shapely. He had tidied the room ready for her coming. The pillows were full.

A cloud breaking into the room had left a neat hole high up on the wall.

"Should we cut off the point of this cone at an angle to the base plane, the resultant shape is an ellipse."

Zuckman's walls are now sixteen metres high. He has a tape measure reaching to where wall and ceiling intersect. The height of the walls is always rising. They have been rising since Ellen left.

The walls are so white they appear the colour of neon tubes. Eric's baby hands are flat on the large desk. The sphere and cone are standing alone with their shadows. The desk lamp casts a harsh sun on the desert surrounding Eric's drawings and formulae. The pages are wasted, containing only desolate scrawls. Drawings of cones and spheres, the sign of infinity. Some of the pages are screwed into balls.

Eric's body is the only real flesh left existing in the room, the rest is simply drawing, a cartoon. Eric can not relate. He no longer takes care to check the height of the walls rising even higher about him.

"The Earth follows the course of an ellipse in its orbit round the Sun. But what interests us here is the point of the cone."

Eric stops writing. On the last page is the drawing of a cone with the tip cut off. The dismembered piece is drawn beside it, bleeding. Only the blood is real, the rest drawing. In the maze of formulae above this is the name Ellen. Ellen equals something.

Eric's face is looking up from the desk. His eyes are moist. The walls are so bright now, he cannot see the ceiling far above him. A set of stairs near the door lead upward. He walks across the cartoon floor, places his sweating pudgy hand on the railing, takes the first step upward.

Ellen's head is at the window, the scarf round her hair. She knocks on the glass but he is far up the staircase now, plodding slowly each step.

She notices blood dripping down the white walls.

My Flat
Mate

Harry was killed by a rolling apple. He was standing on the road outside the car sales yard when it came over the hill. His body was covered in juice when they gathered round to see it.

The apple rolled on though, through a fence into George Pymble's Farm. Nobody would have cared except that George was the last farmer in the world.

Glenelg
Beach

(with photographs and diagrams)

This is us getting into the car. Bernie took it before
we left. Yes, she drove. Look at her gold ear-rings,
her loose fine hair. That backside of hers!

Who could tell what Bernie was thinking? Just
the two of us going off. I often wonder why he didn't
come—he must have known all along. In his car
too.

Bernie's car was the container which carried us
into an afternoon of light. Objects, substance, matter
did not exist (and finally, even she did not exist as
her flesh melted and she became nothing but a shade
of gold), just the light emanating from all. This was
what Monet registered, the master painter of light
who hardly noticed sorrow as he watched his wife
die. He was totally engrossed in the changing hues
of her death mask. I wonder what you'd call that?
Callousness? Obsession? Sensitivity? What?

Heading Towards the Coast . . .

"And what do you desire?" I said to her like a father.

"You," she said, "But how come I'm always involved in triangles?"

"What do you expect? To be whisked away from the matrix of your acquaintances by Zorro on a flaming stallion, and from inside the folds of his cloak, look back to see the friends of your mundane life (left sitting in the sickly yellow light of mundane experience), talking about you, jealous of you. You've shown them!"

Sounds good doesn't it? The Knower (The Real Zorro, Me) thrusting at the adolescent fantasies fed to her by the advertising magnates, to incite her dreams. They give her bricks and tell her to build a castle in the air. How we desire to be saved from the general throng of life, from the greasy sardine-can social set in which we lie. A pity the Fisher of Men has fallen from popularity. His mistake was using a crucifix instead of a Gibson guitar.

Map of Australia:

All this used to be sea, right across Adelaide up as far as the Flinders Range. There's a fault line coming down through here, across the gulf. If that fault line moves, you could expect the sea to come back, with a will. Imagine it, after the onrush, when things calmed down again, sharks gliding through the smashed windows on the seventeenth floor of Adelaide's AMP. In the subconscious depths of some

Adelaide minds, a fear of that tidal wave is continually swaying like a current, annoying the white nerve endings of the brain. Along that mental beachfront, huge dark waters brush against the soft material brain. There're sharks in those waters.

A guy told me the seas off South Australia are the world's breeding ground for the White Pointer.

Sepia:
I know what year it is, but this photo of Glenelg Beach should have been taken at Brighton (England) in 1932. And not just for the sepia effect. This photo's got an English feel about it. Probably, the stone houses along the beach front, the sea wall, stucco change rooms with lime oozing out of the cement, the enthusiasts paddling in the shallows with their trousers rolled up. And least of all this lady's dark sepia grace. The brown sad and serious eyes.

A Problem Concerning the Photographing of Spiritual Visions with a View to Ascertaining Authenticity:
We'd just finished talking and I had gone to walk along the beach alone. She had shown me something of herself, like opening her rib cage and allowing the accumulated tears to rush out over me.

A few minutes later, on my own, I looked out

over the sea and squinted into the light. The sea aglow, the sky flickering like constant lightning.

I wasn't sure if I was going schizoid or coming into Nirvana. The thought also occurred to me that this was the beginning of a tidal wave.

How would you get a shot of that?

The Chemistry and Aesthetics of Alright:
I've developed a means of processing negatives which emphasizes the "mundane aesthetic" in scenes, portraits and landscapes. Take a photo of a grand sunset and it comes out looking quite ordinary. This process is aimed at developing a sense of detatchment in the viewer. The benefit of the process can be seen more easily when one looks at a photograph of a shoe, a tap, or an old cup. One is impressed by a strange quality of existence a tap can assume under this process. One sees the photograph and says "Ah, a tap, yes, taps are alright."

Of course, I expect the advertising magnates to exploit the technique for crass commercial purposes. It's the type of process that'll make the ordinary look really desirable.

Here are some photos developed under the process.

See this one, a character study. Look at him. He's so English, a white shirt and tie, trousers rolled up, paddling around the dead seaweed. And this one of an old woman rolling a stocking back up her leg. She'd been paddling too. I saw her later with a string bag over one arm, and nothing in it but a clean folded tissue. Her body was like a handful of brambles stuffed inside the rag of her dress. But she could walk "alright". She was walking with me along a path that followed the shore.

We talk about the shore, that place where the Antarctic Ocean touches Australia. It's a line that actually doesn't exist. A line on a map but really, down at Glenelg, the little waves come in from miles out over the curve of the Earth, and they play havoc with that line.

And if you look far out to sea, it's all grey. Any minute expect a great white shining ice-berg to break onto the horizon and move slowly toward the line that marks the beginning of Australia. "Alright, an ice-berg's coming," you might say.

This boy was walking up the beach across some stones. I noticed his head like a small wailing machine, a black hole for the mouth. He could wail okay. The rest of his body could keep walking while he did it. No one came to give succour. Not me. He was walking towards me. Notice the "alright effect" here, the lack of succour.

And this little girl climbing the sea wall. The wall which followed the shoreline in an ordinary-following kind of way. She made it up to the top of the wall as I reached her. I'll just step back and get a photo of that.

A little girl is climbing some rocks to the concrete path. The man and the girl reach a point on the path at about the same time. (Approximations see, they're so ordinary.) She brushes off her hands with a self-satisfied grin on her face. The man doesn't care really that she's climbed to the path, it's just "alright", that's what little girls do, and out of habit he says, "good job eh!". She says, "I climbed all the way up there." And indeed, she is okay at climbing.

"Kylie, don't talk to people you don't know," says a mouth from below the concrete wall. Kylie brushes her hands. The man grins at the stupid old bitch.

Beach Girls under the Alright Effect:
Below the path, two females are browning their bodies, lying on the sand. The man looks at the bottom part of their bikinis. Both of the females have lumps up where their legs join together. He knows what those lumps are, but sexuality is softened by the "alright" process. He doesn't even worry about breast content on these two. They can do it. Two lumps of meat can splay themselves out under the sun and go brown.

The man looks at the sea. He makes himself notice the curve on the horizon. He likes the curve though he would like to meet people who had strong arguments in favour of a Flat Earth Theory. He'd attend meetings. Why not? There's something more mundane and "alright" about a Flat Earth than a round one.

He's conscious now he's moving back towards the lady of 1932 sepia. Between them, sail boats glide out over the water, children swim, a yacht anchors a little way out.

The concrete path follows the shoreline back to her. He sees her on the sand, there she is. The long hair, the typical curve of the back. He doesn't want to see her yet. He's still taking "alright" photos. Her sepia features would be an intrusion.

He moves into some shade. Just a quick glance at the map. There it is, Glenelg. There's the line that marks the edge of Australia. She's actually sitting now somewhere on that dark line, yes, he sees a huge black line coming along the beach, roughly following the shoreline. She is coated now in black ink as are half the other sunbakers. Some have dark torsos with untouched legs, others have only been spared a toe.

He waits within the sphere of shade under the tree. Musing, taking "alright" photos of Sunday-afternoon Glenelg.

From time to time he watches the sepia lady. The sea's still there too, rolling in.

Topography:
Her back is small and freckled. The ranges formed by her shoulder blades are extremely mobile and dainty. I noticed all this as I rub oil into the landscape. Up at the back of her neck is a white area where the hair sweeps away. One freckle resides here. For this man, the sea has gone, the rest of the beach fades, I delve into a different part of Earth.

Her thick lips, like two boulders, part and I enter

into the warm light of a new sea. Her waves flow across my body, swallow me down into the ocean bed where I roll like a dead fish, listless in the undercurrents. It may be—in some similar situation —I'd feel more like a flying fish, but not with her. These kisses have the taste of complication. The triangle thing. Lisa and Bernie loom in the skies above us like aerial whales. Someone's pulled the plug out of the bath, the water is sucking away the blood in my heart.

But anyway you can't really do much on a Sunday-afternoon beach, a family scene. This is how I recorded my frustration.

A Short Clip from a Swedish Film on Sex Education: The background is dark blue. A diagram of a penis moving in and out of a vagina takes most of the action. To one side a graph is measuring the relative stimulation levels of both male and female genitals.

On the blue background, a small semen motor is pumping, pumping. Semen comes from somewhere off the screen, through the motor, along a tube into my balls. A red flashing light marks the full capacity my balls can take. It's been flashing now for quite some time as I lie with her on the sand. My motor runneth over with lust. Here I am, unable to empty my balls in the manner to which I have become accustomed.

There's so much these movies don't explain. I'm planning to burst the field wide open: "Follow That

Tube: A Frank and Revolutionary Insight into Sexuality". It'll be a movie that follows my tube right back, from the semen motor, through the cavities of my heart, through galaxies of myself where strange emotional globes turn in slow motion, and finally to the light receptor which resembles an eye. I'll even show a picture of that eye and the dew falling on it, dew from that eerie grey sea which separates herself and myself. It's that dew which drops back along the tube as semen. And those sperm creatures are no dainty sea-bed flowers but deep-sea killers (killing with the passion only lovers can bear), bursting skin and letting blood as they rush along the tube, eager to be first to break from the penis into her silent sea.

It's a heady task, a complex movie, but it's still only biology. There's so much more. I mean, how many people are involved in one successful orgasm, providing material for erotic fantasies and such like, as well as those offering plain old-fashioned support? And, on the other hand, there's all the people we carry inside us (whom we know won't approve, or who'll be jealous) hanging like aerial sharks, raging and voracious, endangering the fragile semen tube.

We swam. There's something about water. It's the same stuff whose multiple fingers reach across the curve of the Earth and brush ice-bergs down below. Whose multiple fingers surround breeding sharks and their offspring. Multiple sacred fingers.

I see her legs in the water before me, I grab her, changing the expression on my face to frighten her, take her deep down in the water with me where my penis will be large and inflated. Michelangelo could paint it. A fierce dark eye, muscles, prominent penis, holding her body which is no hinderance to my on-rushing pace back toward the ice blue sea, miles under.

"Don't. Don't."

"Why!"

"I'm really scared of the sea. Look how far out it goes."

We bought fish and chips at the shop. Broke into some figs, trying to "get off" on their sensuality. (Didn't work.) Took a picture of the sun setting into the sea at the end of the pier. In the foreground, a great phallic symbol, Wakefield written on it. If the sea comes in, that won't fall, merely be surrounded by water and fish. Then, we went home.

Yeah, but before that, before we left the sea completely, she changed colour. She went gold, she grew warm and soft. Her body aged but grew more supple and proud. She was much older than I. One of her eyes explained half the world, the other made a sly warm dance. I was inundated with the gold water of her body. Some people might say I'd fallen for her.

And as we headed back to Bernie in Bernie's car, a huge jet, lights blazing, dropped down through the evening sky, below the Adelaide Hills, waited in the air, suspended low over the city. Imagine it like some great steel god, some strange immense fish moving down to Earth slowly through the dry grey sky, but never, never touching the tarmac. A real life photograph. Perfect.

Real
Australia

When a wallaby's shot, it shudders under the impact
of the bullet. That shudder vibrates through the
biosphere affecting every blade of grass, every
animal and micro-organism, enters the eye of the
rifleman, destroys some part of him.

The wallaby runs, feels a strange wetness rushing
inside, a smell of blood; fretfully realizes its body
is somehow alien, is falling back behind its fleeing
spirit. Kicking and thrashing then on its side, we
see the tender underbelly, the white parts. It loses
camouflage, becomes un-sacred, untidy.

And moving up through the trees into the
biosphere, its spirit soars above the saltbush sea,
curving at the Earth's edges.

The wallaby, rising like a bush pilot, sees the
legendary transparency of the Blue and Distant
Mountains and, chancing to look back to its own
ruined body, its eyes pass over the civilization of
Real Australia—the buildings scattered like freight
dropped from an aircraft, like flotsam in the pure
and magnificent sea.

The Skin of
My Teeth

I wake up, stumble to the mirror and Jesus, what am I lookin at. Some bastard's taken me face during the night, laid a new one on me like a slice of corned meat.

The eyes are familiar, but the rest, looks like some kind a retard's face. I try to peel it off like the top of a meat pie but I'm bloody scared what'll be underneath, probably rats' balls in gravy.

I yank back the lips to get some leverage. Look at those teeth! They're mine. Solid, right into the gums. I remember peeling the skin off em once, it kept smiling at me while I tried to wash it down the drain. Bastard of a smile.

I give this face a proper jerk but she won't budge.

"Hey come n have a look at this mate. Recognize me?"

"Yeah. Gedday."

"Come on, cut the grin will ya. You can see what's happened. Give us it straight. It's ugly isn't it?"

"What's ugly?"

"Me face."

"Yeah, sure, so what's new?"

"It's not me own face is it."

"Looks like you to me mate."

"Have a proper look will ya. The eyes are closer together. It's fatter, noticeably fatter. The nose, just that little bit longer. I've put years of work into the other one, shaving, pluckin blackheads till all hours of the night. No, this isn't me. The whole thing, it's just not me, doesn't suit. See if you can peel it off will ya?"

"Geez, don't ask me to do that, mate. Never know what I'll see, like taking the top off a meat pie. Maybe your eyes'll hang out all over the place."

"Jesus you do it or I'll bite yer bloody head off. I've still got the old teeth yer know."

"That's your bloody trouble. Been biting off heads again have you?"

"No why?"

"That's what makes your face look like that."

"No, look, some cretin laid it on me during the night."

"Crap."

So what does a man do? Accepts a second-class product, shaves it, makes it look presentable, takes it along to the office. Never know what the chicks'll go for. Maybe shove it between a pair a boobs come closing time.

Harlequin

I am a harlequin of the sea. My lips are inches long and useless. I babble above the water and underneath it. Underwater my lips float like lazy fish.

At my belt hangs a large key. I have nothing sacred to keep locked away. While I yearn for an unusual secret, the key remains unused, crusted in part by tiny sea creatures.

My toil involves the forging of glass gimbals— to keep me steady on the tormented waves. Delicate pivots and rings of multi-dimension, they circle high above me, or deep down where the light can hardly come.

There are gimbals sometimes not to be seen, even by myself. I have created some of light; these are delicate indeed. But I am not yet steady. The key still chafes against the body. The rolling sea plagues me.

One more gimbal, of utter darkness perhaps— then I shall be still. And I will unlock the sea.

The Pressed-Flower Posture

My wife is a small woman. The first passions that she fired in me hinged on the fact of her smallness, on my ability to totally envelop her body.

We both enjoyed this imbalance of power though we realized its limitations, the classic Freudian father/daughter relationship.

A year or so after our first meeting she showed me a heavy old book, a family heirloom; squashed between its faded ancient pages were all the small flowers I had ever given her. The juice was certainly gone from them.

I am watching my wife now as she does yoga; small but very supple, almost double-jointed. The arms, outstretched, have the flexibility of a bird's wing. Her hand is dainty, aerodynamic. I imagine her flying, a tiny thing, high in the sky, and she is confident the huge expanses of air will buoy her up. The sky is like a blue father with whom she can play any tricks, never be hurt.

Her posture is tighter now, easily contained. I would choose her as she is now if I wanted her preserved in a glass block. Everything would fit very neatly.

In those early days, when I lay on top of her, kissing in the grass, I was afraid of crushing her. I asked her about this. She said she enjoyed it, she felt like clay being pushed and moulded. And kissing her ears, cute little hairless animals, I'd want to pull her whole head inside my mouth.

Her posture changes. Her face reminds me of a child. Sometimes, so much like my own child, I feel that once she was curled up within my womb, contained there.

And now, her smallness, her helplessness, still bring fatherly affection from me. But at times, I desire to push heavy glass plates over her, to press them down; she, like a flower in the old book. As I press her under the glass with the weight of my body, I see her face, appealing, a silent pleading, unheard from behind the glass.

Pieces for a Glass Piano

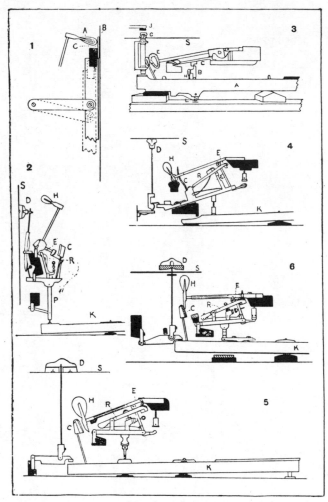

Pianoforte Actions.

1. Celeste pedal, causes the hammer A to strike through a strip of felt, c: B is the string.
2. Modern upright pianoforte action (Broadwood's): s, string; K, key; H, hammer; E, escapement; C, check; R, repetition spring; D, damper; P, prolong. 3. Cristofori's action: A, key; B, hopper; C, escapement lever; D, hammer butt; E, hammer head; F, check; G, damper; H, hopper check; J, damper stop; L, spring regulating play of hopper; S, string. 4. Erard's action (1821), on which all modern grand pianoforte actions are based. 5. Modern grand action (Broadwood's), at rest. 6. Modern grand action (Bechstein's) after the key has been struck. References to 4, 5, and 6: S, string; K, key; H, hammer; E, escapement; R, repetition lever; C, check; D, damper.

Pianos used to be quite popular in the home. By manipulation of the piano machinery (red and green felts, nifty hammers, wooden levers, wires and brass pedals) one could produce music. During the early sixties this was overlooked and pianos suffered.

Elderly women enjoy the traditional and familiar sound of the piano. You can win their hearts by playing the old tunes. They might sing along. You can become popular by playing for them, and make their lives happier for a few moments.

It's possible to learn a tune a day if you don't need to pass exams. A brick room is ideal for the inhibited beginner.

In 1968, pianos were cheap. Their price has steadily increased over the years making the instrument a good investment as well as a dignified piece of furniture.

Pianos were the first machines to be mass produced. Elderly ladies probably don't know that.

A Concise History of the Pianoforte:
The sketchbooks of Da Vinci show that white birds
first imagined pianos. Elsewhere on the same parch-
ment a note, "apples are the essence of silence," and,
at the bottom, a scratching in black ink concerning
the uses of apple juice. Rumour has it that Da Vinci
built a huge wooden apple and fitted it with a
keyboard.

For centuries, folk had confused smooth stream
stones and creamy milk with a faint notion of
harpsichord, but once Da Vinci's discoveries were
accepted throughout the halls of Europe, progress
began toward a clearer formulation of harpsichord
and this was to lead on to pianoforte. But even then,
the decadent French courts related the piano's
ancestors to rich multi-tiered cakes, to garish gold-
leafed trimmings, to lace and snuff boxes. However,
the notion of piano survived.

Moonlight passed across the keys.

Our own century has seen many variations of the
piano:
  (a) The white star-spangled pianos of vaudeville
      quick-buck shows, packed with tinsel to go
      on the road, their tongues hanging out like
      brash alcoholic jokes
  (b) The blues piano shining like a light (contain-
      ing ivory and white birds) in a ghetto of black
      writhing and sad bodies
  (c) The honky tonk, danced on by a wailing siren
      in fishnet stockings
  (d) The baby grand at the Cream Bun Bistro that
      cops a gobful of bra and garter every night.
      And loves it

(e) The piano on whose wood sleazy women singers roll voluptuous curves of flesh
(f) The eisteddford piano backing a choir of prepared-carnation children
(g) The padded grand that's insinuated into the Martini Bar, playing a semi-classical Musak
(h) The Uncle Sam piano sweating out a Dixieland rhythm
(i) The pianos of the sixties which remained silent under the axes of guitar-crazed youths breaking with tradition
(j) The piano in which Yoko Ono (wrapped in a hessian bag) did her thing
(k) That surrealist piece, the baby grand, stuffed with a mutilated donkey
(l) The Beale, which they say is the FJ, the Holden of pianos

Rules for Piano Keepers:
1. Always sit at the piano with a straight back, making sure the hands are washed and manicured. (Strong but tender fingers are required.)
2. Reserve the piano top for special photographs (weddings, etc.) never vases of flowers.
3. Provide the piano with the correct stool, it gives the piece a clean finish.
4. Mice which eat the intricate felt pieces inside the piano should be treated kindly.

Entice them out with a portion of bread dipped in vanilla essence.

5. Never take off all the wooden panels at once.
6. Do not open the top of the piano more than once or twice per year, or something will happen.
7. Small wooden boxes of child things, hidden inside the piano, enhance its magic.
8. Elegant curtains hanging near a piano add to its stillness.
9. Illuminate with candlelight or firelight in the evenings, or by the dusky light of the late afternoons. Never open the piano in the mornings except on rare occasions.
10. Never take a piano to a funeral, particularly as a coffin.
11. Dilapidated pianos, wrapped in green felt, should be carried by hand into the forest, there becoming homes for mushrooms and luminous fungi.

Rules for Glass Piano Keepers:

12. Peel off skin immediately after delivery.
13. Remove all the apples carefully, gently picking them off the finer glass strings.
14. Perspex piano stools tend to scratch.
15. Glass pianos have very sensitive felts. Do not confuse glass pianos with hospitals, the equipment used in laboratories and old

people's homes, or make any other pharmaceutical connection as it may seriously
injure the felts.

16. For best performance, glass pianos should
    be situated in spacious rooms with high
    arched windows showing only the sky.
17. Sit at the piano after dark and under bluish
    light.
18. If the moon should suddenly appear at the
    windows, do not turn to look at it directly.
19. Never use a glass piano as a means of
    frivolous entertainment. Or something will
    happen.

Practice This Easy Piece:
A bag of silent apples is hidden among the roots
of a large tree. A nearby stone looks like a moss-
covered planet. In fact, there is a planet, one million
times the size of the stone, wandering in a distant
galaxy. Everything about the stone and the planet
are exactly the same—except for size.

A shaft of glass limelight breaking through the
treetops catches the stone and illuminates a pianist,
sitting magnificently at a glass grand. The piano
machinery is made from insect limbs. The strings,
distilled from apple juice, move out of the piano and
merge with the burning racing sap streaming
through a tall tree. The pianist is contemplating the
symphony of a distant mossy planet. He knows a
bag of apples has been hidden in a forest there and
his fingers now play the silence of those apples.

Other Australian Fiction Published by University of Queensland Press

Aspects of the Dying Process by Michael Wilding
The Ship on the Coin by Rodney Hall
Peanuts in Penang by David Richards
The Tins and Other Stories by Peter Cowan
The Tidal Forest by Geoff Wyatt
Living Together by Michael Wilding
A Place among People by Rodney Hall
The Fat Man in History by Peter Carey
The West Midland Underground by Michael Wilding
Contemporary Portraits by Murray Bail
Johnno by David Malouf
Flame and Shadow by David Campbell
Walking through Tigerland by Barry Oakley
The See-through Revolver by Craig McGregor

Forthcoming

Gully Wedding by Barbara Hanrahan
Something in the Blood by Trevor Shearston